Monkey Football

By

Bobby Legend

Published through Legend Publishing Company

Book Design and Layout by Mickey Strange:
ISBN: 978-0-9909373-9-5

Introduction

This is a story of humanity, the love of animals, and most of all, the love for football! It begins as an unfortunate way of life for the special people working at the Rwanda Wildlife Preserve and the endangered species roaming its over 200,000 acres. But because of the more than 30 armed security guards protecting the Reserve and the dozen or so animal care specialists, this story does have a happy ending.

The main characters are an American couple who are top-notch veterinarians who volunteer their time at the Reserve once a year for nearly six months at a time. But this was a special time for them, as their family now included quintuplets—all boys—whom their mother had birthed at the Reserve's hospital a little more than two months before. The boys were quite a handful for the couple, especially when emergencies cropped up. And this was one of those times. Their family would soon become a family of six boys, one being a baby mountain gorilla that came into their lives unexpectedly. His father, a silverback!

Chapter 1

On a hot and muggy day at the Rwanda Wildlife Preserve, the Preserve's security guards were fueling up the helicopter to head out for their morning rounds to look for any poachers over the 200,000 acres and to protect the endangered species and other wild animals on the range.

Nearly an hour into their flight, the crew of six flew over a gruesome sight. From above, they saw a troop (also called a family, group, or band) of approximately 20 mountain gorillas, including the dominant male silverback, most likely dead, as he was being eaten and gnawed at by a family of hyenas.

The crew radioed back to their home base and explained their visual sighting! They called for immediate action by the ground crew—a team of 20 armed men, including four trackers. Upon receiving the correct coordinates for the tragedy, the armed men jumped into four different jeeps and headed out to see what damage had been done.

In the meantime, the helicopter crew flew as close to the scene as possible without crashing into the forest. The helicopter frightened the clan (family) of hyenas, causing them to flee. What happened next was a sight to behold!

The helicopter crew knew that the ground crew would need approximately two hours to reach their destination. Once they saw that they had chased away the hyenas and were positive the scavengers wouldn't return, the crew continued on their way, keeping an eye out for any possible poachers that could have caused this murderous destruction of such beautiful and endangered gorillas—all just to cut out and collect the scrotums of the males in the troop to sell to merchants from Asia.

The Asians seemed to believe that gorilla scrotums, once dried and made into a powder, could be mixed in drinks or taken in a capsule to give the taker special powers and a longer life. Elephants and rhinos met the same fate as the gorillas—killed by poachers for their particular body parts—all to satisfy the appetites of greedy Asian merchants.

Be that as it may, the troop of mountain gorillas was known to the medical staff at the Reserve Animal Hospital, where wounded and abandoned animals were helped and cared for. These included baby elephants, whose mothers were shot and killed by poachers for their ivory tusks, while the babies and others in the family watched in terror.

At that time, the hospital was caring for a number of orphaned baby elephants and leopard and lion cubs. The cubs' parents had also been killed by poachers, who then skinned off their beautiful coats.

Now, there would soon be another addition to the hospital zoo, but the little thing was near death, and the crew was not expecting it to survive. It was truly a life-and-death situation.

****

Nearly two hours after they'd received the distress call from the helicopter crew, the ground crew finally arrived at the ghastly scene. They chased away a number of hyenas, especially one that was gnawing on the midsection of a baby lying in its dead mother's arms.

All 24 armed crew members were aware of this particular Troop. A quick count revealed a total of 26 mountain gorillas, including one silverback: eight were bull males, 12 were females, and six were babies. The youngest was approximately two months old.

The trackers could see immediately, based on the many different footprints and bullet casings littering the crime scene, that a group of at least four poachers using AK-47's had brutally killed this troop of mountain gorillas. Most of the gorillas had been hacked to pieces, their heads decapitated, and bodies slashed. The males' scrotums and the females' breasts and genitals had been removed. Only one female hadn't been touched or mutilated in any way, other than being shot in the head as she clutched her infant baby in her arms.

A few of the crew documented the scene and checked each gorilla for manner of death. The last one checked was the unmutilated female lying flat on her back. As the baby was lifted off its mother, it was evident that its midsection and part of its stomach had been ripped apart by hyenas or cut out by poachers. Not a fun way to die.

But dead is dead. And this baby was dead. Or so they thought, until they heard a faint cry and felt movement from this little baby as it took a deep breath.

"We've got a live one!" the crew member yelled to the others in his native tongue.

Three of the other crew members came over to the jeep to help care for the "miracle" baby. They quickly took some clean rags and did their best to keep the bleeding to a minimum.

Within a few minutes, four crew members and the baby gorilla were heading for the local hospital, the accelerator pressed to the floorboard. They notified the hospital staff, warning them to have the operating room ready for the worst.

The baby looked to be about two months old or younger. Even though they were going as fast as the jeep could travel, the ride was very bumpy and scary as they raced to get the baby to the hospital before it passed on. It was constantly going in and out of consciousness, and its midsection was still bleeding profusely, even though they had dressed the wounds as best they could. Finally, after a nearly two-hour harrowing and terrifying ride, the crew arrived with the baby. It was still alive.

Chapter 2

The hospital crew were already outside waiting for their victim. The baby was handed off to one of the doctors, who whisked it into the examining room. The four crew members, having got the little one there in one piece and still alive, were now anxious to get back to the others at the crime scene. They needed to help the others document and collect evidence, just in case the poachers were caught and hopefully brought to justice.

***

The little one was in bad shape. Most of the hospital staff had very little hope for a favorable outcome.

Not only was the baby gorilla in bad shape, but so was the hospital, especially the examining and operating rooms. One week earlier, an electrical fire had decimated nearly all the special equipment in the hospital.

The X-ray and dialysis machines were burned beyond recognition, along with the EEG and EKG machines, and none had been replaced. Most of the equipment now being used had been brought in and paid for by the doctors themselves. They had been able to replace the two electron microscopes lost in the fire as well as basic stainless-steel utensils, such as scalpels, clamps, and other operating tools, and special magnifying eye glasses, adhesive tape, sutures, bandages, and a sterilizer for sterilizing their operating tools used in surgery. The bigger items had been ordered, but had not yet arrived.

The doctors and nurses working on the baby had to play it by ear and work strictly from experience. Ether was the only drug they had to knock the baby out while they examined and operated on it. And to use it, they had to place the ether on a clean rag and then hold it over the baby's nose and mouth. They were working as though they were in the year 1950.

***

The only veterinarians on call at that time were George and Mariam Boyagian, an American couple who had just had quintuplets. As they examined the baby gorilla, they believed it to be about the same age as their quintuplets—two months old. However, until they could clean the wounds and inspect the damage the hyenas or poachers had done, they could not predict a favorable outcome. One reason was that there was no blood to replenish the blood the baby had lost, and even if there had been, they had no transfusion machine, as that too had been lost in the fire.

Once they had the wounds cleaned and examined them, they remained uncertain whether the hyenas or the poachers had been the culprits. They decided both were at fault.

They had no X-ray machine, so knowing the exact sex of this endangered species was impossible to determine. They figured that its scrotum had been torn out for its special powers and taken by the poachers. They believed the baby gorilla was a male.

So, they had to make a small tube from a piece of its backside and attach it to the urinary tract so that it could urinate without a problem. But the Boyagians, as they performed the surgery, weren't sure if the baby would even live through the eight-hour operation.

They had no blood pressure machine—or any machine, for that matter—to help in the operation. The only tools available were the basic ones, such as a stethoscope, which they used to take his pulse by holding their fingers to his little wrists. They had to depend on their experience, and if that wasn't enough, then they had their prayers to fall back on.

***

Many of the hospital workers believed it was a useless waste of time trying to put this little baby gorilla back together again. But the Boyagians refused to give up and gave it all they had. They stopped the bleeding, cut out a small piece of tissue from its backside, and after sewing up the small cut, George sutured the baby's urinary tract to the tube that Mariam had shaped by wrapping it around a small plastic straw, which would be taken out as soon as the sutures dissolved.

The tube would allow the baby to urinate normally, but only if he could beat the odds and stay alive. When he was a bit older, they'd be able to reconstruct his scrotum and missing male parts, but for now he'd have to live with a reconstructed bladder and a urinary tract connected to his new urinary tube. That was, if he was able live through the night.

***

Nearly eight hours later, the operation was complete, and the little guy was still alive and breathing. The next few hours would determine his outcome.

They gave the little gorilla intravenous antibiotics to stop any infections that could arise within the next few hours. They also built a small incubator for the little guy, and after wrapping the little tyke in a warm blanket, they placed him into it and hoped for the best.

He had a slight fever, and after taking a few drops of his blood to check using their newly replaced electron microscope, Mariam noticed he had a strange blood infection. But the fever broke after she switched him to a different antibiotic cocktail, and the infection seemed to be disappearing.

She stayed by his side for the next few days, watching the baby gorilla closely for any signs of failing health. But the baby refused to give up. For the time being, they fed him intravenously along with his antibiotics, which seemed to keep his body fed and his infection in check.

For the time being, he was closely watched by the doctors and staff. After a few days, he was holding his own. After seven days, he was getting stronger—and restless.

He was no longer in shock from seeing his parents and relatives killed in front of his eyes. He was now kicking his legs, wanting to get out of the incubator and walk. So Mariam picked him up, pressing him to her bosom, while he held onto her, his arms around her neck. She thought it was time to feed him from a bottle instead of intravenously, so she unhooked his feeding tube and held a warm bottle of milk to his mouth.

He refused to take the nipple into his mouth. She talked to him like a mother, hoping that he would feel the love and take the bottle. But nothing doing.

She had another idea. She brought him to where her own five boys were busy sucking on their bottles of milk.

The baby gorilla looked in awe at what they were doing. She placed him in between her boys so he could feel the closeness of their bodies and then held the bottle of milk to his mouth. He did as the boys were doing and finally took the nipple into his mouth and began sucking the special formulated milk into his stomach. Soon, the little tyke was holding the bottle himself and sucking that milk into his mouth, as though he were starving.

As the days passed into weeks, the baby gorilla grew stronger and more alert to his surroundings. He was constantly in the presence of the quintuplets, whom he seemed to consider his brothers.

The baby's health continued to get better, and his appetite grew as long as he was in the presence of his brothers. The days grew into weeks, which grew into months.

***

The boys and the gorilla were now inseparable. Six months after his emergency surgery, the baby was once again a healthy gorilla. And just in time.

The Boyagians' time at the Reserve had come to an end. It was time to return to the US once again. But now they had an important decision to make—whether to take the baby gorilla with them to the States. The boys and the gorilla really loved each other. So, the Boyagians made the decision to take the gorilla with them and be his parents, as they had been for all these months at the Reserve.

Chapter 3

After making plane reservations, the Boyagians packed their bags, said goodbye to the staff and security guards, and were driven to the airport. It would be at least another year before they would return to the Reserve and volunteer their time and abilities. But today, the Boyagians had their hands full, traveling on a commercial aircraft with six babies, one being a baby gorilla.

Just getting on the plane with two baby carriages specially made to fit three babies each was a hassle in itself. They were allowed to board the plane first, so the flight attendants could fold up the carriages and put them away. They put the babies in the back of the plane, where the seats could be folded down like a bed. This allowed three babies to lie on each bed, with pillows placed all around them so they wouldn't fall.

The female attendants looked in amazement at the babies. Then they noticed that one of the babies was a gorilla. But they didn't freak out. They actually thought that the baby gorilla was even cuter than the quintuplets.

The flight attendants were as helpful as they could be. One even sat in the back, watching the babies as the parents slept. Most of the time, the babies slept. But when they were awake and hungry, the attendants pitched in to feed the horde their specialized formula and even helped with changing the diapers.

The attendants got a kick out of feeding the baby gorilla. They loved the look he gave them, with his big brown eyes and his hand reaching for their faces. They were tickled pink with all the babies.

The Boyagians experienced the same kindness and consideration on all their air flights. After the eight-hour flight from Rwanda, they landed in Egypt, where they had to spend the night after going through customs. The airline paid for the hotel room for the tired parents and their six babies.

Then it was off to Morocco—another eight-hour trip. That flight went the same as the first. The female flight attendants were as nice as ever and helped the parents with the feeding and diapers.

They had no trouble with customs in Morocco, but customs in the UK was a different story. The UK customs officials would allow the baby gorilla to come into their country, but it would have to be placed in quarantine for ten days. The Boyagians thought this was outrageous and were at their wits' end.

Fortunately, a supervisor overheard the problem with the baby gorilla, and took into consideration that the

Boyagians' next flight from Gatwick Airport was only two hours away. The supervisor overruled the customs officer and allowed the baby gorilla into the country without any restrictions, but it had to be out of the country and on the plane in two hours.

The Boyagians thanked the man, gathered their brood, and continued on their way. However, before they could leave, the supervisor told them he would take them to the airport in the company's van, as it would be long and wide enough to fit the two extra-large baby carriages and nine people.

In all, it took three days riding in planes, starting from Rwanda, before all eight family members landed safely in America. The trip had been a long one, with four plane changes—the last being at La Guardia Airport in New York. However, upon landing at La Guardia, they had a little trouble going through customs with their newest family member. But that was short-lived, as they had all the correct papers for the baby gorilla, as well as new passports for the quintuplets who had been born in Rwanda and now had traveled with their parents to the US when they were seven-and-a-half months old.

Finally, after a four-hour layover, they were on a plane heading to Los Angeles, California. Five hours later, all eight family members had landed safely in Los Angeles. Once there, Dr. Boyagian called his brother, who owned a small moving van big enough to carry two large baby carriages and nine family members.

***

Once everyone was in the van, the talk turned to football. This family, including Dr. Boyagian's brother, were fanatical football fans—especially Los Angeles Rams football fans. George and Miriam had even named their boys after many Hall of Fame football stars. Unfortunately, only two of those were Rams stars.

The first-born Boyagian boy was named after Jerome "The Bus" Bettis, a Hall of Famer running back for the LA Rams before being traded to the Pittsburg Steelers. Their second-born was named after Dallas star and wide receiver Michael "The Playmaker" Irvin. The third boy was named after Hall of Famer star and quarterback for the New York Jets and the LA Rams "Broadway" Joe Namath. Their fourth boy was born about two hours after his brothers and was named for Hall of Fame star linebacker for the NY Giants Lawrence "L.T." Taylor. And the last of the quintuplets, who finally came out nearly three hours after the first born, was named after the Great Hall of Fame running back for the Chicago Bears Walter "Sweetness" Peyton. And last, but not least, the sixth and final brother was named after the Dallas Cowboys defensive end De Marcus "Tank" Lawrence. And the names fit perfectly for the little guys,

15

especially the baby gorilla, whose nickname became "Tank."

Mariam had wanted to name the new family member after San Francisco 49er offensive tackle Trent "Silverback" Williams, to honor the tyke's father. But after a short argument with her husband, she conceded and went with "Tank." But they really wanted to wait to name him until they could see what type of personality he'd have, hoping it wouldn't be one of depression and antisocial behavior, but one of happiness and gentleness. They hoped he would forget the nightmare that he had been part of.

Well, so far, so good. It seemed that Tank had forgotten his past as he'd shown no sign of nightmares. The Boyagians believed he loved the new world he was now living in. And as far as Tank was concerned, he was just "one of the boys." The Boyagians thought the same and couldn't be happier. "He *is* one of the boys!" they thought.

*****

Finally, they reached their home. They were met by the family's caretaker and nanny, whose nickname was "Hazer," short for Hazel. She helped take the kids out of their carriages and place them each into their own crib. She was taken by surprise as she counted six kids and then realized that one was a baby gorilla. It had tightly wrapped its hands around her neck and did not want to let go, did not want to get into the crib, but only wanted to feel the warmth of a human body. Hazel thought it was the sweetest thing, but she finally placed him into his own crib.

***

Once they were fed and had emptied their bottles, sleep followed soon after. The light in the room was off, but a nightlight was left on so Hazel the nanny could watch them on a computer using the kiddy-cam located in the eye of a teddy bear sitting on a shelf in their room. And in just a few minutes after shutting off the light and closing the door, one of those six silently crept out of its crib and hopped into another. But seeing they were nearing eight months old, the mischievous one was none other than the newest member of the family, Tank! He was the only one of the brothers who could walk and climb at this young age.

Hazel was going to go into the room and place him back into his own crib, but she saw that he only wanted and needed the closeness he would have gotten with his mother. Now he was getting it from his brothers. She decided to let it be and let them sleep. She watched as the little guy put his arm across his brother's chest and cuddled, falling fast asleep.

***

The next morning, once diapers were changed and bodies fed their specialized formula, all six boys were put on the carpeted living room floor so that they could crawl and build up their arm and leg muscles. However, the hairy one refused to stay down and wanted Hazel the nanny to hold him close to her chest, as his mother had done in the wild.

Hazel tried repeatedly to put him down to be with his brothers, but he wanted none of that. He wanted her, to be close to her, as though she was his surrogate mother. If she put him down, he would "oooh" and sit at her feet, grabbing her leg until she again picked him up and let him feel loved.

As she sat, he hung onto her, not wanting to let go. But for feeding time, she placed him on a special bed with all his brothers—it was an enclosed crib that was actually a bed with walls.

Once the boys finished eating, sleep occurred almost immediately. This gave the Boyagians a chance to sleep away their jet lag.

After making another 24 bottles of formula, the Boyagians went back to bed and left Hazel to look after the brood. She was happy to do it.

She treated those kids as though they were her own, including the new addition. Hazel smothered Tank with love after hearing what had happened to his family and knowing that he had witnessed the massacre and the deaths of his mother and father and all his sisters, brothers, and cousins. So the nanny paid special attention to Tank.

***

It took a week before the jet lag disappeared, and now the Boyagians were ready to get back to work. Mariam and Hazel made 24 bottles of formula for the kids' daily intake of liquid food, and the two veterinarians were ready to see how their staff had managed their business while they had been away.

The Boyagians had volunteered their time and expertise every year at different African Wildlife Preserves in Congo, Kenya, South Africa, Rwanda, and many other places over the last ten years. But Mariam wasn't like other veterinary doctors—she had a disability. However, that didn't stop her from reaching her goals in life.

At the age of seven, she had been in her house when it blew up from a gas leak. The concussion had blown out both her eardrums, leaving her deaf. So, beginning at age eight, she was taught sign language at the California State University, Northridge (CSUN) for deaf children and adults.

She graduated high school at age 16. She was a straight-A student and was accepted to medical school at the University of Chicago with a scholarship, all expenses paid. Upon graduating, she moved to Palo Alto to Stanford University for her graduate work in medicine as a Dr. of Veterinary Medicine because she loved animals. She especially enjoyed working as a veterinary intern for the San Francisco Zoo, which was only 30 miles from her dorm room in Palo Alto. After six years, she graduated with honors—Magna Cum Laude, which is Latin for "with great honor."

Mariam began teaching her six boys sign language just days after they were born, but in earnest at four months. None of the boys were deaf, and all could speak grunts and groans. Their hairy brother took to those sounds almost immediately, as they were similar to the sounds he had heard from his little cousins and his now-dead mother.

The hairy tyke was constantly drinking his formula because, in the wild, he constantly drank his mother's milk and would have done so until the age of three. But he was now getting a crash course and soon would change over to human baby food when the boys did. However, he would still be given his bottles of formula. The Boyagians would give him formula until the age of three, just like he would get from his mother.

Chapter 4

Everything was fine at the Boyagian Veterinary Hospital, but profits had gone down the past year. Therefore, the Boyagians decided it was time to return to work and see if they could turn things around. It wasn't easy, to say the least. They worked 18-hour days and were exhausted by the time they returned home, which meant they had little time for their babies. Many a night, they microwaved their meals and then went straight to bed.

It was too hard to care for six boys, particularly when one needed the special attention that only a mother could give. Therefore, Hazel became the surrogate, holding Tank almost continuously, except during bottle feeding with his brothers in their big bed and when sleeping. Sometimes, he would become curious and want down while watching his brothers crawl on the living room floor, playing with their toys (which were nearly all mini-foam footballs). They bit at them, put them in their mouths, or hit their heads on them when their little arms gave out. "Bam!" The head would hit the football. That was Jerome "The Bus" Bettis Boyagian. He was the clumsy one. They each had their own idiosyncrasies. Michael "The Playmaker" Irvin Boyagian was the thinker. Michael liked to stare into space, always thinking about football. "Broadway" Joe Namath Boyagian was the bashful one. He would always look away from the person speaking baby gibberish. Lawrence "L.T." Taylor Boyagian was the quiet one. And Walter "Sweetness" Payten was the fast one. He was the fastest crawler out of the bunch, crawling from one end of the living room to the other and back in a matter of minutes. Afterward, he was worn out and ready for bed, as were all the babies.

The months passed quickly. The babies, including Tank, grew at such a fast pace that new clothes had to be purchased monthly and sometimes even weekly. Tank was now 15 pounds heavier than Jerome, who was the heaviest of his four brothers and the tallest.

Hazel had a number of tasks to do each and every day, and the most important was to teach the kids sign language when the parents weren't able to teach them how to sign. For one reason or another, they left that job to Hazel, their trusted 32-year-old nanny. Another important job for her was to make 24 to 36 bottles of formula each and every day. Soon after, this became feeding the growing boys at least three to four times a day while allowing the parents—if not too tired from work—to feed them at least once a day. Lately, that had been once a week.

For the time being, housework was left to the two staff members: one was the landscaper and the other cleaned the 6500 sq. ft. five-bedroom, five-bathroom house. The pool cleaner was only called to clean the pool once every two months due to its lack of use.

***

The months turned into years, and at least once a year, the Animal Control people would come to the home or business to complain and harass the Boyagians. Animal Control stated that they were just making sure the Boyagians' license to keep Tank in a residential neighborhood was up to date, claiming they worried about the safety of the neighborhood's children and families. But nothing ever came of these checkups as Mariam's sister was married to Mayor Samuel Johnson, meaning that the Boyagians were good friends with the mayor. The harassment stopped once the Mayor was made aware of the situation.

Tank grew at an incredible rate of speed. Each year, he gained 20 pounds or more. By age three, he was already 105 pounds and had a reach more than a foot longer and taller than his brother Jerome, who was second in this statistic at a svelte 48 pounds and a reach a foot less than Tank's. All the boys were bigger than average, taking after their 42-year-old father, who was 6'7" and 340 lbs.—the total package. George was what women died for! And two of Mariam's brothers and one uncle were also above average in size and weight, as all were 6'4" or better and in the 300+ lb. range. All were huge men. So the boys were following in their father's and uncles' footsteps.

As the years went by, the boys could all speak sign language fluently. This included Tank, who had picked it up quite easily and, having learned it, drove the others crazy because of all the questions he asked. He wanted to know the names of everything in sight—birds, other animals, and just anything that caught his fancy. So, they used flash cards that showed pictures of different animals, including mountain gorillas.

The boys' birthday was coming up—and so was Tank's. They were having a problem with Tank, though. In the wild, Tank would have nursed from his mother's bosom until age three. Hazel tried weaning him off formula and onto a diet of solid foods, such as fruits and vegetables and baby foods that came from a grocery store and were sold in glass jars.

The boys had been eating that type of food for years already, whereas Tank only drank formula out of a bottle. He refused all other types of food. He would try baby foods out of a jar and bits of different fruits, but ultimately rejected them all.

The Boyagians were disappointed at this turn of events and wondered how much longer it would be before Tank would eat the same food as the boys. The answer came soon after their birthday celebration—a trip to the zoo.

There, Tank witnessed other mountain gorillas across the moat eating the same type of baby food concoctions his brothers were eating. He decided it was time he tried it. This time, Tank was first in line and was given a choice of a bottle of formula, a cup of chunky baby food, or both. Tank now surprised everyone by taking both the cup of chunky baby food and a bottle of formula to wash it down.

***

At age five, all five boys were allowed to play midget football. Tank sat on the sidelines in the stands during their practices and games.

One day, while Tank was watching the team practice, Animal Control and ICE agents came into the stands. They threatened to quarantine Tank for 21 days and then have him deported to Kenya rather than his homeland, Rwanda.

The ICE agents went out of their way to terrorize people, whether innocent citizens or not. ICE put them into the same category—guilty until proven differently, which could take months or even years.

Luckily, the Boyagians had stopped by the field to see how their boys were doing, as all five were playing for the Lincoln Falcons. Jerome was playing running back. Joe Namath, of course, was the quarterback. At nearly four and a half feet tall, he overlooked the opponents and field, giving him and the team an advantage to dominate opposing teams! His brothers played both offense and defense.

The Boyagians were so proud of their boys, especially knowing that they could speak English and "sign" fluently. When among other boys their age, they spoke English orally. Tank understood English, but he just couldn't verbalize the language. But when around their mother, or others who were deaf, they spoke by signing.

The Boyagians spotted the Animal Control agents harassing Tank, who sat there as though he didn't have a care in the world. An agent poked him in the right bicep repeatedly with his index finger, but Tank ignored the man.

Seeing this, the Boyagians immediately shouted to the agents to stop the harassment! Seeing the Boyagians, the two cowardly agents ran away like criminals, not wanting to get on the bad side of the mayor, who could fire them in a minute. The ICE agents watched the game.

***

During football games, Tank was the silent mascot for the Lincoln Falcons. It was ironic—a gorilla dressed as an eagle that flapped its wings each time they scored into the end zone. He did a great job while watching the game intently, keeping an especially close eye on his brothers and Joe. If Joe was "on" and he hit his receivers, the team was unbeatable. If he wasn't, Jerome, Michael, and Walter would have to pick up the slack on the offensive side.

While playing in a playoff game, Michael and Walter played an excellent offensive game, scoring a total of 24 points combined, while L.T. and his defensive teammates held the opponents to six points. The five-year-olds played as good as determined NFL players, or at least they thought so. Joe Namath completed 18 passes for a total of 220 yards, with only one interception. His brother Michael Irvin had 10 receptions for a total of 120 yards, while Walter Payton had a total of eight receptions for 100 yards and another 56 yards on the ground, while Jerome Bettis ran for a total of 72 yards, while brother Lawrence Taylor had six quarterback sacks. That win helped thrust the Lincoln Falcons into the Eastern Divisional Championship Game.

That game was only two weeks away. The kids playing in the game were nervous, to say the least. That special day finally rolled around, and the Lincoln

Falcons won that game 10–0. Next up was the game against the John Glenn Owls for the State Championship. That was what the Falcons strived for.

That was why these five-year-old kids worked out in the school's gym for two hours every morning before school started and again two hours after school closed. The kids had bodies that Adonis would have been proud to have. This was Midget Football, and those kids didn't mess around, boy!

The Falcons won their game against the Owls for a chance to play in the National Championship Game against the Chicago Canaries. It was a tough, hard-fought, exhausting game for both teams, and the Falcons eventually lost 6–3.

Chapter 5

As football season ended, the boys suited up for their next favorite sport: hockey. All five boys played both hockey and basketball during the fall and winter. Tank also watched their practices and games intently from the stands, trying to figure out how to play the two games. Sometimes, at hockey practice, Tank was allowed to join them as the goalie. He was perfect for that position.

After finding hockey kneepads, chest protector, gloves, and a mask, and putting them on, Tank was ready to try his hand at goalie. The opposing team members shot pucks at him at 60 mph, but Tank was so huge that he hid the net, making it that much harder for them to get the puck past him.

Shot after shot fell to the ice, bouncing off his chest protector and knee pads. Not one shot got past Tank, no matter what the other team tried. Shooting the puck into one of the corners didn't work. Tank covered the whole net. Some players thought it was unfair that Tank was that big. But nothing in the rules could stop him from playing if he wanted to. Other schools would cry foul, and the case would most likely end up in court, but no school could afford or want that—or the publicity.

Tank was great in just about all sports, except swimming. He was exceptional in basketball, as the Midget League used the normal distance of zero to eight feet from the ground to basketball hoop. Standing under the hoop, Tank could stretch his hands up over his head, stand up on his two feet, and, without even leaving the floor, he could dunk the basketball without any problem. If allowed to play in the league, Tank would be an asset for any team or school.

The school's basketball coach tried to get Tank on the team, but was denied. He would try again the next year, and if that didn't work, he would try again the following year. He vowed to keep trying until Tank was allowed to play. Even if he wasn't allowed to play in middle school, he would hopefully be allowed to play in high school.

Tank's adopted mother and brothers wouldn't give up. They would get him on their team "come hell or high water!"

The local news team heard about the "basketball and hockey playing mountain gorilla" and interviewed the school's gym coach, who coached the football, basketball, and hockey programs. And on that same day, they interviewed Tank's five brothers.

When the news affiliate's anchor heard that the gorilla could answer questions in sign language and his brothers could interpret, he wanted to speak with Tank pronto! Tank was called over for his interview, along with his brother Jerome as interpreter.

Standing together, Tank was asked questions by Bobby Legend, the anchor, and the questions were answered in sign language by Tank, while Jerome explained what Tank was signing. The anchor was flabbergasted as he watched the gorilla answer the questions quickly and correctly, as Jerome told him in English what Tank had said.

Tank was asked which sport was his favorite, as he could clearly play all three sports. Tank replied that he also could play soccer, but football was his real love, and he liked watching his brothers play the game.

When asked if he would like to play on his brothers' team, he got excited and replied with a smile and a happy sound that erupted from his mouth.

Jerome handed Tank a mini rubber football that the team used in games. "Show this guy what you can do with the football," he said with a smile, knowing that Tank could throw it a mile with a perfect spiral.

Tank smashed the ball in his hand to get a feel for it. He then threw it with a perfect spiral for more than 40 yards.

The anchor stood awestruck at what had just happened. Tank was a natural, and only five years old.

He asked Jerome if he could watch Tank at a hockey practice in the near future. Both Jerome and Tank agreed, but for another day.

Many schools tried to entice Tank's adopted parents with briefcases full of cash and gold and with diamond-encrusted jewelry. One tried to bribe George with an 18-carat Rolex watch ringed with diamonds around the face and one diamond in each number. However, schools that had asked and tried to bribe their way into the parents' good graces were denied, at least for now.

All the schools wanted Tank to join their football teams because they saw that he could run, throw, hit, and tackle with the best of them. However, Tank's five brothers weren't to be included in the deal. The problem that the schools ran up against with that was that they had no one who could "sign" with Tank.

They needed someone who could communicate in sign language, or Tank would be lost on the field and wouldn't know the plays. Now, he had Jerome or another brother who could interpret for him, but since the schools were not interested in the other Boyagians, they were denied access to Tank.

***

As the brothers grew, so did Tank—much bigger and heavier than all the brothers combined.

Tank continued to watch his brothers play football from the sidelines. Meanwhile, five different schools agreed to take a case to court to get a ruling regarding whether Tank could play on their teams. The case wasn't dismissed outright and weaved its way through the court system. After five long years, the judge finally ruled that if the schools didn't object to Tank joining either of the five schools that had brought the case, then he had no objection either. It was now up to the schools.

When Tank heard of the favorable ruling from Jerome, all the brothers, including Tank, jumped for joy. Next season, Tank could play on the school team and would, with luck, help the Lincoln Falcons win a championship. However, to do that, he had to first enroll in school.

When the principal allowed Tank's membership on the football team, he also signed Tank up for school classes. Tank was placed in the fifth grade with Miss Mable, who taught sign language to her deaf students. She believed Tank would be a good example for her other students and would encourage them to learn sign language.

Chapter 6

A month after Tank started school, Miss Mable took her class to the zoo to see the animals. When Tank and the class passed the enclosed mountain gorilla grounds, he thought he saw his relatives in that enclosed area surrounded by a moat. He was saddened at being away from his mountain home in Rwanda.

Miss Mable was having a hard time keeping all the kids from wandering off and trying to keep them all in one group. Before she knew what was happening, Tank suddenly crawled over the high brick wall, jumped into the moat, and dog paddled to the other side. Crawling out all wet, he quickly shook himself off.

A female gorilla approached him. Within seconds, the dominant male, a silverback, came running out of his lair and confronted Tank with a lot of huffing and grunting. Standing upright on both legs, the silverback began pounding his chest with his fists.

Tank wasn't fazed and remained calm. He talked to the male first in his native tongue, which was a series of continuous grunts. He then gave him the sign to "relax."

Whatever Tank did seemed to calm the silverback gorilla down. Each began to touch each other with their fingers, and they seemed to become friends.

The gorilla troop congregated around Tank. He signed to them and used his grunts and native tongue, seemingly telling them what his sign meant. All of them, including the silverback, listened and watched intently to what Tank was trying to teach them.

Within just a few minutes, many in the troop were trying to make the sign themselves, although they were basically just parroting Tank. Nevertheless, Tank refused to give up, and slowly a few of the females seemed to be aware of what Tank was telling them.

Tank continued trying to teach his new friends how to sign, but the zookeeper forced Tank out of the area and back to his classmates. He was saddened to leave, but he made loud guttural sounds that his new friends reacted to happily. Tank basically told them that he'd be back to teach them sign language.

The zookeeper saw the kind of hold Tank had on the other gorillas, and he couldn't believe his eyes. Tank was just like a teacher teaching his pupils how to "sign." The zookeeper was amazed at what he saw and asked Miss Mable if Tank could come back another time.

"You'll have to ask his parents," said Miss Mable.

"His parents can sign too?" asked the zookeeper.

"No," Miss Mable replied. "His parents were killed by poachers in Rwanda, but human parents adopted him, brought him to the United States, taught him how to sign, and now he's one of our pupils at Lincoln Elementary School."

"I'd like to see if Tank can teach sign language to my mountain gorillas!" the zookeeper said with enthusiasm. "I believe we have a few that are smart enough to learn how to sign, especially two of our females. Tank reminds me of that mountain gorilla Coco. She knew how to sign, but they never had her try to teach other gorillas."

"I don't know if Tank can teach any of your gorillas," Miss Mable said, looking dejectedly at the zookeeper. "He won't be able to spend much time with them. I mean, if he comes here one hour every six months, what can they learn?"

"Yeah, you're probably right."

She continued. "I mean, Tank was raised with his five human brothers, and at four months old, he was taught how to sign for a few hours every day, after eating and sleeping."

The zookeeper seemed confused. "Why were he and his brothers taught how to sign?" he asked.

"Tank's adopted mother is deaf. She and her husband are veterinarians and volunteer their time and abilities six months of the year at different game reserves in Africa. That's where they adopted Tank after tragedy struck his troop. All his troop members were massacred by poachers. However, I will speak to the Boyagians for you about Tank visiting your zoo from time to time," she promised.

"I'd appreciate that. Thank you. Tank is one amazing animal. More like a human than a gorilla."

She laughed. "Well, that is from living with the Boyagian family and five brothers. He's just one of the boys to them."

Before leaving, Tank signed to the zookeeper that he had "enjoyed his time" visiting with his relatives and that "he'd like to do it again" from time to time.

Miss Mable told the zookeeper exactly what Tank had told him.

"I'd like that," the zookeeper told Tank. Miss Mable repeated his words in sign language to Tank.

With that, Miss Mable rounded up her class and got them back on the bus with very little trouble.

Once back at school and in class, Tank and Miss Mable began speaking in sign language to each other. Miss Mable then used sign language to ask a few of the girls if they understood what she and Tank were saying to each other. Only one of the five girls replied that she knew what they'd said.

Most of the 12 students in the class weren't as smart at using sign language as Tank was, but they were there to learn. Miss Mable made Tank her assistant so he could teach half the class how to sign, while Miss Mable taught the others. Both used flash cards that showed an object and then showed the sign for that particular object. That had been exactly how Tank had learned—using flash cards.

Once school was over, Tank waited after class for his brothers so they could all go to football practice together. Broadway Joe was the team's quarterback, Michael and Walter were receivers, Jerome was halfback and Lawrence played defense. L.T. played linebacker, while Tank played defensive tackle.

Tank was so huge and tall that he towered over all the other team's players. They couldn't get past him. If they threw the ball, Tank slapped it to the ground. If they ran the ball, Tank was there to tackle the runner. Nothing got past him.

After a few of the players on opposing teams were hurt just from Tank's weight falling on top of them, the coaches of the other teams began to complain to Tank's coach and, later on, to officials of the league.

With Tank's team winning game after game and their opponents not scoring a single point, the other coaches began to get louder and louder, complaining that

Tank was much bigger and heavier than their kids and should play on a middle school football team and not on an elementary school football team.

The Boyagians took these coaches' words to heart. The principal at Lincoln Elementary agreed and promoted Tank to the eighth grade, while his brothers stayed behind at Lincoln. However, without his brothers, Tank refused to play football or any sports unless his brothers were playing with him. After just one month, Tank was back in his fifth-grade class with his deaf friends.

Tank agreed to sit on the sidelines while his five brothers played the game. Even without Tank playing, the Lincoln Falcons still won every game they played. Their wins took them to the divisional championship game against the Wildwood Warriors, which they won handily 36–7.

Their next game was for the national championship against the John Glenn Owls. The Falcons' opponents were much bigger and heavier, as most were sixth graders, whereas the Falcons' players were fourth and fifth graders.

The game started terribly for the Falcons, as the Owls went ahead in the first minute of play by returning the punt for a 65 yard touchdown run. They kicked a field goal for the extra point. The Falcons had no field-goal kicker. Their legs were too small to kick a field goal, so they had to run it into the end zone from the twenty yard line for their extra points.

After the opening kickoff, the game went completely out of hand for the Falcons. By halftime, the Owls had the lead 36–0.

The Falcons couldn't do anything right. The five brothers played their best, but it wasn't good enough. They had to do much, much better in the second half.

The Falcons received the ball on their thirty yard line. Jerome caught the ball, but just as he started running, an Owls special team player hit him hard, which made him fumble the ball. An Owls player recovered it on the Falcons' twenty-eight yard line, and their first play scored a touchdown on a quarterback sneak play when the quarterback faked a handoff to the halfback but kept the ball himself. L.T. nearly tackled him on the twenty-five yard line, but the Owls player was six inches taller and nearly 100 pounds heavier than L.T. He simply shook off L.T.'s tackle for the touchdown. The score was now Owls 42, Falcons 0.

Tank was upset because the Owls players rubbed it in about the Falcons being losers. Jerome looked at Tank and called out his name from the bench. When he saw that Tank had seen him, Jerome signed to him, and within seconds, Tank was sitting on the bench wanting to play.

The coach had a big decision to make—lose the game by a landslide or play Tank and hope he could make a difference and stop the Owls from scoring again. The coach decided he would play Tank on both the offense and defense to help get the team going again.

The coach ran into the Falcons' locker room and found Tank's football uniform in his locker. Before the season started, they'd had to get one from the Detroit Lions that would fit Tank. He quickly ran it to the Falcons' sidelines and helped Tank suit up.

The Owls coach was surprised when he saw Tank run onto the field for the kickoff. He didn't complain, but instead yelled at the Falcons players, "Tank can't help you now."

But Jerome caught the ball on the kickoff and handed it off to Tank. Tank ran the ball from the Falcon thirty yard line all the way to the end zone, while three Owls players jumped on his back at the same time. They couldn't stop him. He carried them like he carried the football—with ease. The Owls players weren't even noticed. The score was now 42–6. After Tank carried the ball into the end zone for the extra point, the score was 42–7.

The Falcons kicked off. Once the Owls had the ball, they tried to run in the opposite direction to where Tank was heading. But Tank was too fast for them, and he caught the runner. With one swoop of his massive arm, he knocked the ball out of the runner's hands, picked it up, and took it into the end zone within a matter of minutes for another touchdown. Only four minutes of the third quarter had passed. There was a lot of time left on the clock. After the extra point, the score now was Owls 42, Falcons 14.

The Falcons kicked off once again. The Owls' fastest runner caught the ball, but Tank honed in on him and hit him with his body so hard that the runner flew three feet in the air and landed approximately 12 feet from where he had been hit. Tank picked up the ball and ran it once again into the end zone. After making the extra point, the score now was Owls 42 and Falcons 21.

***

Before the Falcons could kick the ball off, the third quarter ended. That left only 10 minutes in the game. The Falcons still had their work cut out for them.

The Owls coach was up in arms over Tank playing in the game! He hadn't thought much about it when his team was ahead 42 to 0. But now that the Falcons were only three touchdowns behind, he was suddenly upset. So much so that, in between quarters, he ran onto the field and complained to the referees about Tank playing in the game, saying, "He shouldn't have been allowed to play in the first place."

The Falcons coach told the refs that Tank had never been taken off the players list and that list had been given to them before the game started. The refs checked the list and confirmed that the Falcons coach was correct. The argument about Tank playing was over.

***

The Owls coach stomped off the field and back onto the sidelines, muttering to himself all the way. Minutes later, the game continued—it was now the fourth quarter, with ten minutes left to play.

The Falcons kicked off to the Owls, and it was "déjà vu all over again." An Owls player caught the ball and tried running away from Tank and toward the Falcons end zone, but to no avail. He couldn't get away from Tank.

Tank hit him so hard that as he tackled him, the ball came loose, and Jerome was there to pick it up. Jerome ran it into the Owls end zone for another touchdown, with a little more than eight minutes to play. After the extra point, the Falcons were now only 14 points behind.

The Falcons kicked off again, but this time L.T. smacked the ball out of the Owls runner's hands. He picked the ball up and started running, but was cut down on the Owls forty yard line.

Broadway Joe called the next play. "Let's give the ball to Tank and let him run it into the end zone."

***

The two teams faced each other with desperation in their eyes and on their faces. Numbers were called. The center hiked the ball to Broadway Joe, who in turn handed the ball to Tank. But instead of running the ball as played, Tank saw that Walter Payton was down close to the Owls ten yard line. There was not an opposing player in sight.

So Tank let the ball fly high into the air in a perfect spiral that hit Walter perfectly. Walter caught the ball and ran the ten yards for another Falcons touchdown.

The extra point was good, as Broadway Joe ran it in with a quarterback sneak. That play was as good as any NFL team could have done. The score now was Owls 42, Falcons 35.

The tables were turning. The Falcons were in striking distance to either tie the game or win it outright—and let the Owls coach eat his words. The Falcons needed only one more touchdown for a tie and two to win, but they only had three minutes left to play. And it would be the Owls' ball on their thirty yard line.

The runner fell to the ground at their forty yard line, just a second or two before Tank would have hit him. Their second play was a pass to their best receiver, but the pass went too high. The Owls quarterback had thrown it over his receiver's head.

The player at the right place at the right time was none other than L.T. He picked the ball off in the air and ran it back for a touchdown—a sixty yard run into the end zone! A minute later, Tank ran the ball into the end zone for the extra point. Only one minute and twenty-two seconds was left in the game that was now tied 42–42.

The Falcons had to kick off to the Owls. Their only hope was that Tank or another Falcons player could get the ball back in time to score another touchdown for the win. Tension was heavy in the air. Both coaches were biting their fingernails down to their nubs. The game was down to the wire. Who would win was anyone's guess. The Falcons were desperate to win it after losing the first half by a score of 36–0.

And here was the kickoff. The Owls runner misplayed the ball, and it went high over his head near the Owls twenty yard line. It was a tremendous kick for the Falcons, the best one all night. With Tank clearing the way for the Falcons, Michael was closest to the ball. Picking it up, he started running for the end zone, with a clear path for the win.

Suddenly, Michael stumbled and fell. He kept the ball in hand, but he was still three yards from the end zone, with only eight seconds on the clock. They had time for just one play.

The coach called a time out and huddled the team together on the sidelines. He gave them a pep talk. "Okay, kids," he said. "It is time to man up. Tank, you're the man. Broadway, hand the ball off to Tank and let him run it in for the touchdown. Let's give the Owls coach something to really yell about. He's a whiner. Complaining to the refs that Tank was ineligible. But we showed him! Now, let's win it for Lincoln Elementary school!" he yelled, jumping up and down in a frenzy.

The Falcons ran onto the field. After a brief huddle, they got into formation, ready to hand the ball to Tank and for him to run it into the end zone.

However, the Owls knew that they would give the ball to Tank, as the Falcons had just done so for the extra point. The Owls set their defense up all on one side to bring Tank down before he could get into the end zone.

But Broadway Joe called a different play at the line and called an audible. The play was called, the clock started, and Broadway faked the ball to Tank by putting the ball into his stomach, but taking it out without the defense noticing.

Broadway Joe hid the ball to his side. Meanwhile, Walter was all by himself, running to the left end of the end zone. With the defense tackling Tank at the two yard line, Broadway threw a quick pass to Walter for the touchdown—with no time left on the clock! The Falcons won 48–42!

The Owls coach ran over to the Falcons coach, who assumed the Owls coach was there to congratulate him and his Falcons team for the comeback win. But instead, the Owls coach began yelling, "I'm going to get Tank kicked out of the league!"

So much for good sportsmanship. The Falcons coach just shook his head in dismay, but the incident didn't stop him from celebrating with his team for the win.

"You guys just won the national championship title," he told them, with glee in his voice. "You guys are destined for greatness. And Tank, I'm going to give you a good supply of bananas and bamboo shoots. Congratulations, guys. You've made my day!"

Jerome signed to Tank what the coach had said. Tank was happy for the coach. In a state of celebration, Jerome petted and patted Tank on the head. Tank loved it, and let out a happy high-pitched laugh.

Chapter 7

Once the celebrations died down, the volume went up. Coaches from five different schools complained to the school board about Tank. Once again, Tank was the talk of the town but not in a good way.

He had helped win a National Title for the Lincoln Falcons, the first time in Lincoln Elementary fifty-year history. Tank had put Lincoln Elementary on the map, so when coaches and principals complained to the school board, the local newspapers picked up the story. Within a day, national papers from coast to coast picked up the story that five schools were suing a mountain gorilla named Tank that spoke in sign language. And played football.

The papers ran the story for days. Some, like the New York Times, New York Journal, LA Times, and AP, had their reporters come to Los Angeles to interview the Boyagians and Tank. Reporters and journalists from across the nation and around the world wanted to interview Tank. Many were also fluent in sign language.

The television crews associated with those newspapers and with TV stations from public and cable affiliates set up cameras across the street from the

Boyagian home, just waiting to get a glimpse of the "new boy in town" on film. Tank even appeared on the front covers of magazines like People, Vanity Fair, US Weekly, and Rolling Stone, as well as sports magazines, including Sports Illustrated, Sports Weekly, Sports World, School Sport, and Lindsey's Sports. Sports Illustrated titled their article "Monkey Football," with Tank's photo underneath the title.

***

The football season was over. Now, it was hockey and basketball season. The news hounds even followed him to the hockey arena to watch him play hockey with his five brothers. Tank couldn't get away from them. They followed him into the dressing room and watched him dress up in hockey gear. Then they went and sat in the stands to watch him play goalie.

Sports illustrated and Sports World, along with the LA and NY Times, had their photographers take photo after photo of Tank taking hard shots from his brothers. Not one shot made it into the net. Even the coach tried to get a puck past Tank, but he couldn't do it. Not a one. The coach shot puck after puck, with many reaching speeds of over 100 mph. Tank either just let the pucks bounce off his protective gear, or he simply swatted them away, knowing they wouldn't make it into the net.

After seeing this, the reporters were in awe and amazed at Tank's abilities. And Tank was only a fifth grader.

***

The AP took the story internationally, and the Swedish, Icelandic, and Russian ice hockey coaches showed interest in Tank for possible future contracts. However, when they found out that any deal made for Tank had to include the five brothers, they lost interest. Those coaches and teams were only interested in Tank.

The Russian coach cared nothing about the brothers, nor was he concerned about Tank only being in the fifth grade. He wanted Tank now! And he was willing to do anything, legal or illegal, to get Tank into Russia and to convince him, one way or another, to play for the Russian hockey team. However, the Russians knew that if they tried, Tank wouldn't go easily. They were sure about that.

So the Russians sent a four-man hit team to Los Angeles to apprehend Tank and bring him back to Russia by any means possible. They would tranquilize him if need be, put him in a cage, and fly him back to their homeland, Mother Russia.

In the conference room at their hotel, the Russian hitmen put their master plan together. But after checking out Tank's surroundings and home, they found that Tank was in the public eye more than they had anticipated.

They would have to figure out a different plan if they wanted things to go on without a hitch—and without ending up in an American prison. They also found out too late that the Boyagians had hired a 12-man security team to watch over Tank and their five boys, due to many threats of beatings and even death. Deep down, the Boyagians knew that Tank would protect his brothers with his life. Having the new 12-man security team at the ready would keep any and all people with hate in their hearts away from their loved ones.

The most the Russians could do was follow the reporters and camera crews to the hockey arena to see for themselves if the trip was worth it—if what they had seen on videos of Tank playing different sports was true, and if hockey was one that Tank excelled in.

After watching Tank for 20 minutes swatting and kicking pucks away and blocking them with his chest protector and face mask, the Russians couldn't believe what they had seen. Not one puck got past Tank and into the net.

After the practice, the Russian coach gave Tank's brother Jerome his card and said, in his strong Russian accent, "The hairy one is very good hockey player. A great goalie! We want him play for us in Russia, maybe in a few years. Please tell them to think it over."

Jerome shook hands with the coach, and that was the last time the Russians were seen anywhere near Tank or the boys. That was one headache that the Boyagians did not need. They could relax for now, until the next time a problem arose.

***

The Russians returned to their homeland, but evil came back into the lives of the Boyagians and Tank. Hockey coaches from around the world weren't the only people who wanted Tank for themselves.

A more criminal element from Asia landed in Los Angeles, intending to kidnap Tank and sell him at an auction where billionaires from more than fifty countries, including China and Southeast Asia, would participate and bid against each other for the right to lay claim to the endangered species.

Many of the bidders were into monkey brain consumption—the eating of a live monkey's brain while still in its living body. Some Asian countries considered it to be a delicacy. Others believed it to be an act of cruelty. The monkey or ape in question would succumb to death after so much of the brain was consumed.

The Boyagians knew nothing of this ploy until the FBI showed up on their doorstep. The agents informed them of a site on the Dark Web and traffic on the airwaves, meaning that the kidnappers' phones had been listened in on. The FBI had intercepted the kidnappers' six team members and had taken them back to FBI headquarters to interrogate them. When the agents were satisfied with their answers, the kidnappers had been put on a plane heading back to their home of origin. The agents warned them that if they returned and were caught, they were promised a long prison term.

***

In the meantime, Tank and the boys practiced hockey, because the league games hadn't started yet and wouldn't for another two months. Basketball was now the sport of the land, and Tank and his brothers played for the Lincoln Falcons.

When the Jefferson Generals team members and their coach saw that Tank was playing, it was a given that the Falcons would win by a landslide, with Tank making every basket. The Generals coach therefore refused to put his players on the floor unless Tank sat out the game. The coach also mentioned to the refs that their case with the school board hadn't been resolved and that the refs needed to disqualify Tank from playing in that day's game. The refs told him they had no cause to suspend Tank from the game and that the coach needed to get his players on the floor or forfeit the game to the Falcons.

The hard-headed coach for the Generals refused to put his players on the floor unless Tank sat out. As a result, the refs had no choice but to disqualify the Generals and forfeit their game to the Falcons.

The crowd was happy with that assessment, but Tank and his teammates were far from happy, as they believed this was just the start of things to come regarding Tank playing basketball.

***

Tank was now bigger than life itself. He had become a celebrity and was becoming an asset to humanity. The media and the mayor gave thanks to the Boyagian family for doing such a great job with their adopted son.

The government, however, was of a different opinion. They believed Tank was getting more publicity than was needed. They wanted to take Tank away from his adoptive parents and five brothers to probe and study him to see what made him tick.

The Boyagians were at their wits' end dealing with the government, so they hired what was supposedly the best law firm in the state. The firm had never lost a case against the government and were masters at animal law to boot, fighting on the side of endangered species. They were so good at their profession that when they pleaded their cases in front of the Supreme Court, they always won.

The firm had pleaded two earlier cases as one because their clients were two different zoos, three thousand miles apart. The zoos had been fighting to be allowed to cut the horns off their white and black rhinos. Although this seemed like an act of cruelty, the zoos indicated that it was necessary because poachers would climb over the walls of their outdoor enclosures during the night and steal the horns, usually killing the animals in the process. The Supreme Court had ruled in their favor 9–0. They had won hands down. They were two for two.

The Boyagians were therefore fairly certain that the lawyers could quell the vitriol and threats that the government spewed trying to get Tank into their protective custody. Indeed, the government didn't have the proper paperwork, like an arrest warrant. So the Boyagians' lawyer filed a writ to stop the government from harassing their client.

The writ stopped the government in its tracks. But the government threatened to appeal the verdict.

Chapter 8

ue to the case against Tank, he decided to forgo his sports play, take a break, and go back to sitting on the sidelines. He continued to play sports with his brothers, but not for any teams. He played just for fun. He was still allowed to practice with the hockey team, but he sat in the stands for football and basketball. That's the way it went for the next few years, as the boys entered middle school and then high school, with Tank taking his sign language classes and continuing to learn the alphabet that his brothers had been teaching him in their free time.

***

Over the years, thanks to his brothers, Tank's prowess for sports was still in his blood. He proved it every chance he got, whether it was practicing with the high school football team, on the ice with the hockey team, or on the basketball floor playing his kind of basketball. Tank was still the man! And he continued to bring a few minutes of fame to their City of Angels.

***

Time flew by! Tank's brothers and the Los Angeles Romans High School football team were playing for the

National Championship against the Redondo Beach Sea Hawks—an old and local rivalry.

An hour before the game was to begin, Tank was allowed to go onto the field to be with his brothers until game time. He would then return to the stands and watch the game from there.

Sports agents were also allowed onto the field before game time to mingle with the players and try to get their commitment to sign a contract with them for representation for any and all dealings with sports teams' management.

While Tank stood in the end zone with his brothers, a football suddenly landed near his feet. Without thinking, he picked it up, felt it with his hands, and brought it up to his nostrils so he could smell the smell of new pigskin. He loved that smell! He motioned for his brother Walter to go out for a long pass.

Walter ran as fast as a race horse, and before he knew it, he had crossed midfield and was nearing the twenty yard line. Tank let go with a mammoth throw. The pass was long and high and had a perfect spiral. It landed in the end zone and into the midsection of Walter's stomach.

Tank had thrown that pass with ease for more than 100 yards, from end zone to end zone, without breaking a sweat. Suddenly, the Camera-Tron flashed onto the stadium screen and showed a replay of Tank's amazing pass. The crowd went wild.

At that moment, the sports agents smelled money. They turned their heads, straining to see who had thrown that football from end zone to end zone. They needed to speak with that person ASAP. They were stunned when they found out that that person wasn't a person at all but a mountain gorilla. They absolutely couldn't believe it. But they soon came to their senses.

It didn't seem to matter to those money-hungry sports agents that the "person" they wanted to sign to a contract was Tank—a real live mountain gorilla. They didn't even know if he would be allowed to play in the NFL, but they didn't care. Put enough money into the mix, and anything was possible. They were confident they could fix that problem when the time was right, once they had Tank under contract and under their control.

Three agents walked onto the field and into the end zone, asking the other players to point out who had thrown the long pass. They pointed to Tank. The agents acted surprised that Tank was a gorilla, but no matter. They were mesmerized by what they had seen. They had never seen such a strong arm throw a perfect spiral pass. They wondered if Tank could do that again.

Jerome signed to Tank, explaining what the agents had said. Jerome then picked a football off the ground and handed it to Tank, signing him to "throw the ball" to Walter. Walter was in the opposite end zone, over 100 yards away, talking to a rival player.

Tank threw the football like he was swatting a fly. As it passed through the sky like a bullet looking for its target, the football actually made a whizzing sound.

Walter wasn't aware that Tank had thrown the ball and was still speaking to his rival. Suddenly, the ball hit the ground a few feet away from Walter.

The agents couldn't believe that a gorilla could throw a perfect spiral pass for more than 100 yards. No human could throw a football that far. They wanted to sign Tank to a contract that instant. Each pulled one from their jacket pocket and shoved it into Tank's face, hoping he would sign it. He did give them an answer, and it was in sign language. He basically told them to "get lost."

Jerome told the agents what Tank had signed to them. Tank's words angered the agents, but the smell of money was too strong, and they refused to take "no" for an answer.

Each agent left their card with Jerome, hoping that they could talk Tank into signing on with one of them.

The same sports agents had also heard that Tank was just as good at hockey and basketball as he was at football. Sports companies were competing fiercely and vying with one another to secure exclusive contracts with Tank.

However, they soon found that they would also have to include his adoptive parents as his representatives and management team because they represented Tank in photo shoots with the top sports magazines, such as Sports World, which had put Tank's photo on their front cover with the caption "Football Phenom!!"

The agents at the High School National Championship game soon met weeks apart with five different NFL team general managers to express their belief in a player that came to the game only once in a lifetime.

"Won't be another like him for five thousand years," said Jon Love, sports agent.

That was about right. If any one of those guys could pull it off and get Tank signed with an NFL team, it would be nothing short of a miracle.

Soon after the agents spoke with the General Managers, they visited the NFL Commissioner, Roger Goodell to get his opinion on the question at hand.

Jon Love put the question to him. "Roger, is it possible for a mountain gorilla to play for an NFL team? I mean, if he was good enough to make the team."

Goodell looked at Love as if he was crazy, a downright lunatic. "Are you serious, Jon? A mountain gorilla playing professional NFL football? Come on, Jon. Who put you up to this?"

"Roger, I'm not kidding!" Love replied. "Haven't you been reading the newspapers and sports magazines? This ape is stupendous at football. And not just football. He also plays hockey and basketball. The darn thing is great at all three of those sports, like no other." Love pointed to the other two agents. "One of us wants to sign Tank—that's his name—to a contract and then get him an NFL contract. And we need you to amend NFL's bylaws, if needed, so that Tank can play football. He'll blow the lid off NFL ratings. He'll be football's new Caitlin Clark, but even bigger."

"And he wouldn't need to go through the draft," added Tommy Paulson, one of the other sports agents. "He could come on as a walk-on."

Goodell pondered the question of a mountain gorilla playing for an NFL team. "Anything's possible," he declared. "I'll have to get all the teams' owners in one small room," he added. "Get them drunk and then put the question to a vote mentioning that Tank would be an asset and the best promotional gimmick to the game of football. An added bonus is an estimated 100 million dollars to each team's bank account that was fortunate to play against him."

"And the owner that signs Tank to their team will be a godsend," admitted Jack Carson, the third agent. "Because, over the last 15 years, and especially the past year, Tank's already gotten millions of dollars in publicity. That'll equate directly to the team he selects. And if we can pull this off, Tank will most likely sign with the LA Rams because his adoptive parents, along with his five brothers and their nanny, are all fanatical Rams fans. So, the Rams will have an edge over the rest of the teams in the hunt."

"Okay, guys," Roger said. "I've heard what I need to hear. I'll make a decision and let you know what I decide. I'll look into this ape named Tank."

"Oh," Love interjected. "One thing we forgot to mention, Roger, was that we saw Tank throw a perfect spiral pass over 100 yards from end zone to end zone. It was an incredible thing to see."

Goodell just let out a sharp laugh, shaking his head in disbelief. "Okay, okay. Get out of here, and let me make some phone calls. This dilemma is intriguing. Let me see how the owners feel about the subject, and I will get back with you."

"Well, thanks, Roger," said Love. "If you can get all the owners into that small room, ply them with alcohol and then preach to them that it is in their team's best interest and the league's best interest to allow that big ape to play the game of professional football. We're counting on you, Roger. There will be a big bonus in it for you if you can pull this off. Say, at least a cool 10 million dollars or more, all in cash and under the table. You do that, and we'll get him signed," he added. All three agents nodded in agreement.

"We need to hear something soon on Tank," Jack said. "I forgot to mention that Tank's as good in hockey as he is in football. We also have a meeting with NHL Commissioner Bettman next week, and I'm sure he's seen the publicity Tank has gotten recently playing goalie. When the three of us watched him practice with his five brothers, not one shot got past him and into the net. He's huge and nimble and can actually skate. He's an all-around athlete. He dominates every sport he plays. In football, he can throw a pass more than 100 yards; he can run with the best of them with an unbelievable speed of 3.8 seconds for the 40 yard dash, and it takes at least five to six defensive players to bring him down, but usually he carries them on his back and around his legs across the goal line. Tank is incredible."

"To be honest with you, Mr. Goodell," Love admitted, "we would rather see Tank in an NFL uniform than an NHL uniform. Heck, he might even end up playing for the Russians, and we wouldn't want that, would we, Roger."

With that said, the three agents shuffled out of Goodell's office, hoping to hear that Tank would be allowed to play professional football.

Once that subject was settled, the next step for the agents would be to get Tank and his family to agree to a contract. That would be as big a problem as amending the NFL's bylaws to allow a gorilla to play the game of football. But with enough money thrown around and in the right places, anything was possible!

Chapter 9

In just a few days, the five brothers would be heading off to college to play football for UCLA, each with four-year scholarships. They were given full rides to play college ball, but Tank wasn't allowed to go with them. This would be the first time he had ever been away from his brothers for any long period.

His adoptive parents promised to take him to visit his brothers on weekends. They hoped their promise would quell Tank's anxiety about missing his brothers. But most days, Tank was depressed and downright unhappy. Then the day finally arrived, and the five brothers were on their way to college.

They said their goodbyes to Tank and promised him that they'd return to visit as much as possible. Tank was saddened and began to cry real tears. They each gave Tank a hug before getting into their car.

With Jerome behind the wheel, they waved goodbye to their parents and especially Tank. They knew that he'd be unhappy seeing them go and then not being around them like he had been since he was a baby.

***

Tank's adoptive parents quickly recognized how sad Tank was. To brighten up his days, they allowed Hazel to take him to the zoo to visit with his gorilla friends. However, Tank told the Boyagians and Hazel that he didn't want to go to the zoo, signing that it was because the gorillas at the zoo "don't like me." He also added, "And they're stupid and don't want to learn to sign."

"You'll change your mind once you visit them and make friends," Mrs. Boyagian signed back to him.

Tank didn't want to argue, and gave up. He finally agreed to visit the gorillas at the zoo.

For the trip, Tank was given a brand-new backpack. He noticed it was the same color, type, and size that his brothers had been given a few days before to carry their books in.

They had filled their backpacks with books, but Tank filled his with bottled water, flash cards, and different types of juicy fruits to be eaten by himself and his gorilla friends. He hoped to teach them to sign so they could have real conversations with each other using a human form of communication, but with the touch of gorilla.

Hazel brought Tank to the zoo three times a week for a few hours after school and on Saturday and Sunday for four hours or more.

The zookeepers kept their eyes on Tank and his interactions with the other gorillas in the open enclosure, especially the silverback. The big male stayed close to Tank for some reason, acting like Tank's protector. Tank, however, needed no protection. He was as big as the silverback and just as strong, if not stronger. Tank could take care of himself.

The silverback seemed curious about what Tank was doing with the flash cards. After a while, the silverback was sitting with the others, directly in front of Tank. He didn't want to miss anything.

Tank grew fond of the silverback as the male kept the others quiet, in line, and in one close group facing Tank, so he could teach them how to sign. Tank used the flash cards as a way to get through to them, hoping they could see a correlation between the picture on the flash cards and the "signs."

Tank remained patient with his new students, hoping they would catch on sooner rather than later. It took seven or eight visits before most of the gorillas finally caught on to what Tank was trying to teach them. They finally matched the pictures on the flash cards to his "signs."

The zoo's personnel couldn't believe what they were seeing. Tank was teaching his class. When Tank came to visit, the gorillas stopped what they were doing, came over to him, and sat down when Tank signed for them to do so. It was as though they were in school to learn, and Tank was their teacher. The zookeepers believed it was no less than a miracle what Tank had accomplished.

***

Tank was a very happy camper while he was at the zoo teaching class. But as soon as he returned home, he again became depressed. It had been a little over a month since his brothers had left for college. Tank wanted to visit them and told his mother so in no uncertain terms. She agreed and promised Hazel would take him to visit his brothers the following weekend.

Before the trip, Tank had to tell his class of students that he wouldn't be visiting them that weekend because he had to visit his brothers at college. While he was away, he wanted his students to speak by signing with each other. He left the silverback in charge to make sure they continued learning how to sign.

Many in the class were visibly upset at Tank's news and began making loud screeching sounds, while doing a dance with arms raised. These actions showed they weren't at all happy with Tank's decisions—naming the silverback as teacher and Tank leaving them. They did not know if he'd return to teach them again.

However, Tank wasn't at all concerned. All he had on his mind was the trip to see his brothers for the first time since they had left home for college.

***

The trip finally came to fruition as promised by his mother. Hazel had made the two-hour-long trip with Tank to the building at the University that housed his brothers. All the brothers came out to meet Tank and showed their excitement and affection at seeing him again.

Many of the students walking to classes and seeing Tank did not know what to make of it. They wondered if a circus was in town, or possibly if he was a pet of one of the students. They put that idea out of their heads, figuring that the ape was too big to be someone's pet. But their wondering stopped when Tank walked with his brothers to their rooms.

The five brothers had two adjoining rooms and were suitemates. The college paid special attention to their football stars, gifting them with extra-large rooms with kitchenettes included and all the amenities. A rollaway bed was brought in for Tank so he'd feel comfortable sleeping and feel right at home.

Tank was only to spend fewer than three days with his brothers. Hazel would come that Sunday night and take Tank back home so he could get to school the next morning.

When the brothers had heard that Tank would be coming to visit, they had planned their whole weekend with a list of things to do with their hairy brother. One of those "things" was to show him off to their Sigma Alpha Epsilon fraternity brothers at their frat house during their keg party.

They had plenty of time before the party. The boys took Tank with them wherever they went, to show him off. He was a crowd favorite, and the center of attention. Tank actually enjoyed the attention but wondered what all the fuss was about. He was just "one of the guys." Or so he thought.

That night, at the keg party, the beer and hard liquor was flowing like Niagara Falls. It wasn't long before the fraternity brothers took a shine to Tank and began giving him drink after drink, whether it be hard liquor or glasses of beer.

Tank's brothers weren't keeping that close an eye on him as they danced and talked to many of the beautiful women in the crowd. So, at that moment, their minds were concentrating on the women and not on Tank. They believed he could take care of himself, if need be. But they soon found out that they were wrong.

They were also wrong in thinking that they could trust their fraternity brothers with Tank. By the time they found Tank, he was sitting on the couch drunk as a skunk. The brothers weren't too happy about that. Now, they had to get Tank home without any problems. However, they soon found out that that would be extremely difficult.

Tank didn't want to leave and kept "stuttering" with his signing until he became angry with himself and his brothers. He threw his drink and then broke the arm of the couch trying to get up but fell back onto it.

Soon, Tank was so angry that he started throwing tables and chairs and anything that was nearby. He roared and beat his chest, showing he was "king of the jungle."

His brothers had never seen him like that. They had never seen him upset to the point of destroying things. They had to get him back to the dorm before the cops were called.

Too late.

***

Within minutes of Tank's destructive rampage, two cop cars, with four cops with guns drawn, came into the frat house to find out the problem. They couldn't believe what they were seeing—an extremely large gorilla sitting on the couch, stone drunk. They thought the frat brothers had stolen him from the zoo and ordered them to return the "ape" to where they had gotten it. But the cops soon learned that he was the adopted brother of the University's football stars. When his name was given to the cops, they finally realized exactly who Tank was.

They learned that he was a "star" in his own right, and that many professional sports teams were wanting to sign him to a contract.

One of the cops ran back to his car, grabbed a magazine with Tank's picture on the cover, and brought it into the house to show it to his partner.

"This is him," the cop told his partner, showing him the magazine's cover. He handed the magazine and a pen to Tank, hoping he would sign the cover.

Tank took the pen from the man's hands, and using what he had learned from his brothers, he did the best he could while still drunk. He signed his name in the form of a picture of a mechanized Tank.

The party was over once the cops showed up, as nearly all the guests ran out of the house, fearing arrest for underage drinking.

Before Tank could fall asleep from his binge drinking, the cops offered to take him and his brothers back to their dorm room without any more trouble.

Once they had gotten Tank into the back of the cruiser, the other brothers jumped into the two cars and were soon heading in the direction of their dorm room.

The cops even helped walk Tank to their room. Once Tank was in his bed, the brothers thanked the cops for their help and said their goodbyes.

That Sunday morning, everyone awoke with severe hangovers, especially Tank. He asked his brothers why he felt so bad. Jerome signed the answer, "Drink," holding a glass to his lips. Tank remembered and just held his head in his hands, shaking it in disbelief at his actions the night before.

Broadway Joe dropped two tablets of Alka Seltzer, an antacid, into a glass of water and handed it to Tank, indicating that Tank should drink it. "It will make you feel better," he signed to Tank.

Tank did as told and drank the water. He signed to his brothers that it made his nose itch.

The rest of the day, they stayed in their rooms and relaxed after such a drunken fest the night before. Tank had only a few hours before he had to leave for home.

***

Sunday night came faster than expected, and Hazel was expected soon to pick him up. Tank was extremely happy to see and be with his brothers again. He didn't want to leave, but both he and his brothers had to go back to school the following morning.

However, before leaving, Tank and his brothers made a pact that they wouldn't talk to anyone about the party, especially the drinking. They promised one another that their parents would be spared embarrassment.

Hazel knocked at the boys' dorm room. The time had come for Tank to return with her to his home. He was saddened to leave, but he knew that many more visits were in the future. That thought would brighten up his ride home.

The brothers gave Tank a group hug before helping him into the front seat of the car and placing his seatbelt around him. Tank signed to Jerome and his brothers that he could put the seatbelt on himself. "I'm not child."

Tank slept for most of the ride back home. He was still hung over from all the alcohol he had consumed the night before.

Once home, he kissed his mom on the cheek and grabbed his father's arm in an affectionate way to show his love to them. He then grabbed Hazel's hand as she walked him to his bedroom. He climbed into his bed and waited for Hazel to bring him a warm bottle of milk to help him sleep. Before long, he had finished his milk and dozed off to sleep until morning.

***

When Tank entered school, the principal called him into his office to tell him that they were moving him from tenth to twelfth grade because of his incredible work teaching other gorillas how to sign. He would graduate high school in less than nine months.

Tank was flabbergasted, to say the least. He was happy with the promotion to the twelfth grade but wondered if they were trying to get rid of him. He shook that thought out of his head as soon as he thought it.

Once school let out, Tank had Hazel drive him to the zoo to show his students he had returned. He wanted to see what they had learned while he was gone.

When Tank showed up in the enclosure, his friends hooted and hollered and screeched for joy, while "dancing in the streets!" His students were hungry to learn. They were all over Tank, petting and rubbing his back in enthusiastic joy. Tank, with the silverback's help, was able to get them all to sit for class. After a few minutes, they were seated in front of him, waiting for their assignment. But before Tank could begin teaching them, the group's attention was diverted by a bird perched on a limb in a nearby tree. One in the group pointed to it and made the correct "sign" and then shuffled through the flash cards until a picture of a bird was shown. He signed, "Same."

Tank signed in reply, "Yes." He knew then that his students finally understood what he had been trying to teach them.

The caretakers for the gorillas couldn't believe what they had witnessed. Tank had actually taught the zoo gorillas to "sign," and they weren't just parroting or copying him. They actually understood him.

So the teaching continued. Tank showed them flash cards with different objects and animals. He had shown these same cards over a to his students, but for the first four months or so, they really hadn't understood what Tank was trying to teach them. Now, however, they did.

And they wanted to learn more and more, naming each and every flash card—not the name that a human might give them but what they were called when they had lived in the wild. For example, an eagle shown on the flash cards was called "Big Bird," a hawk was called "Mouse Killer," an elephant was called "Big Ears." These names were spot on, according to these mountain gorillas.

Chapter 10

The Los Angeles Zoo's hierarchy heard what Tank had accomplished in just a few months. They were particularly impressed to find that even when Tank was gone, his students continued to teach each other to sign and would tell one another the names of the animals on the flash cards and would correct each other if they were wrong. They were actually communicating with each other in sign language and showed a level of intelligence equivalent to a nine- or ten-year-old human child. Possibly even older.

These observations gave them the idea to tell other zoos in the US and around the world that, for a nominal fee, they could teach each and every gorilla that was sent to them to sign within a six- to 12-month time period. They even guaranteed it.

The nominal fee, as explained in the contract, was needed only to cover the feed for each animal sent. It wasn't meant to make a profit. Most of the plants, shrubs, flowers, and fruits consumed by the zoo animals were donated by a variety of companies and grocery stores. Thus, depending on the number of gorillas sent, they would need to increase the amount of food substantially to keep the animals healthy and well fed.

The zoo's offer was heard around the world. At first, other zoo directors didn't believe what they were being told. Then, they saw an article by the local paper about a famous mountain gorilla that was teaching sign language to other gorillas. Once that article circulated among different zoo hierarchies, the zoo officials no longer thought the idea was a farce. They realized that something rang true in the story.

So, after a Zoom meeting, 52 zoo directors from the US and around the world all agreed to take the Los Angeles Zoo up on its offer and send them their gorillas to learn how to "sign."

Within a few weeks, gorillas were being sent to the Los Angeles Zoo from all around the world. China sent the two that they had been given from Rwanda 20 years previously. Zoos had been given mountain gorillas from three different African countries—Rwanda, Congo, and Uganda. The gorillas had all been trapped in the Albertine Mountain Range.

Over three decades, North American countries like the US and Canada, and a number of European countries, like Belgium, France and Italy, to name a few, had been gifted mountain gorillas at different times depending on the governments' goodwill. These actions had depleted the mountain gorilla numbers to such an extent that the gorillas were now an endangered species. The African countries now guarded their gorilla troops from anyone wanting to take them or kill them. They were especially on the lookout for poachers—considered the worst kind of humans.

Too many gorillas had been killed by poachers or had been stolen from their troops by previous governments and given away. However, with the help of a dozen or so zoos, mountain gorillas had procreated at an amazing rate, producing an average of two babies each year per zoo for the last 20 or 30 years. Those gorillas were donated to zoos that had no gorillas but had built new enclosures in the hope that, one day, they would get a pair of gorillas that could procreate. Their wishes were almost always granted, and most zoos that wanted gorillas for their main attraction got them.

The LA Zoo was soon filled to capacity with 30 new mountain gorillas sent there to learn signing plus 14 of their own.

***

Tank had his hands full trying to teach gorillas that weren't interested in learning to "sign," as many of them disrupted the class Tank was trying to teach. His first and original class that he'd taught were wanting to learn more from Tank, but the "newbies" wouldn't allow it.

Tank asked the silverback to help him get the group in order. It took some doing—a little pushing and shoving and bullying—but the class of 44 were eventually in one close group and finally began listening to what Tank had to say.

The newbies were dumbfounded and confused. Most just stared into space, chewing on roots and flowers.

***

The local news media was approached by the LA Zoo to do another story about Tank and all that he had accomplished. The LA Times agreed, and their front page headline read: "Sports phenom teaching gorillas from around the world to 'sign'." Below the headline was a head shot of Tank and his cute face. Then came the article, which gave a full account of the thirty gorillas sent from 27 different countries and the program that was giving the Los Angeles Zoo international recognition and fame.

Soon after, the international news media picked up the story and sent their journalists and camera crews to the Los Angeles Zoo to get a heart-warming and heartfelt story about Tank, the docile and loving gorilla.

One of the journalists from Australia was so enamored by Tank's abilities that he boasted for all his peers to hear, "If Tank wasn't so hairy, one would think he was a human." He added, "He's got a brain, a heart, and a loving personality. I just wish more humans were like Tank. We'd have a much better world."

Many in the reporter's group of peers agreed with him about Tank, but just as many laughed at the thought of Tank being "human."

Tank, however, found the cameras, journalists, and reporters upsetting. He didn't understand the intense attention he was getting. He believed this to be "déjà vu all over again." He remembered that he'd received a lot of attention in his younger years, but he'd thought little of it then. He'd always thought that the main attention and attraction had been the quintuplets—his five brothers. Tank had always thought of himself a side show. Now, he couldn't understand the media's infatuation with him.

Soon, all the intense pressure placed upon him began to take its toll on his health. He had to get away for a while from all the lights and cameras and crazy interviews with reporters, who asked crazy questions for their viewers around the world, like "Do you remember what it was like living in the wild?"

Tank would answer that question by admitting he couldn't remember anything from that time as he'd been only two months old. But the reporters wouldn't stop asking stupid questions like, "Do you remember your real mother and father?"

Tank would answer "no" and would explain that he was told they were killed by poachers when he was two months old. He kept trying to get the part about him being only two months old through their heads, so they'd stop asking him questions about jungle living. He'd been too young to remember anything, and he really had no wish to remember that part of his life.

***

Soon, Tank was being bombarded with so many ridiculous and stupid questions that he refused to answer them. The whole farce truly began taking a toll on his health. The stress caused him a lot of anxiety and sickness, so he and his nanny Hazel decided it would be a great time to visit his brothers again. That particular weekend was "opening day"—their first football game of the year. All five brothers were starting—three on offense, one on defense, and one playing both offense and defense.

***

Tank was very proud of his brothers and what they had accomplished, as he rooted for them and their team from the stands during game day.

He wished he could play the game again, but he hesitated, knowing what he had gone through playing midget football for Lincoln Elementary School and then playing during middle school at Adams Junior High. The humiliation of being suspended from playing football after being a defense witness against five different school districts that wanted to ban him from playing sports in their districts had never left him.

Before that case had gone to trial, Tank had decided to retire from sports—much to the detriment of his teammates and schools. The trauma that had begun in his midget football days and followed him through middle school made him quit playing sports, especially football. Being sued was the end result of being an outstanding football player and basically great at whatever sport he played. He was a "natural."

He had continued to play sports with the neighborhood kids, but that was far as it went. It saddened him that he no longer had that camaraderie of his teammates, and he missed that "winning spirit."

***

Now, in the stands watching his brothers play, he was pleased when they decimated their opponents—the #2 team in the country—with a score of 42–12. Their opponents had been lucky to get those 12 points.

When the game was over, Tank's brothers motioned for him to join them on the field. They put a football in his hands and told him to throw it like he'd done years before.

Tank did as told and threw a perfect spiral pass from one end zone to the other—over 100 yards. He hadn't lost his touch.

The camera crew had pointed their cameras directly at Tank as soon as he walked from the stands and came onto the field. They showed Tank's 100-yard pass.

The announcer told the TV viewers just how special that hairy ape was. He then schooled his viewing audience about this particular species of gorilla.

"What you are witnessing," he explained, "is a special and endangered species of *Gorilla berengei berengei,* which is the Latin name for his species. His family is Hominidei, his genus is *Gorilla* and his subspecies is *berengei,* which means Tank is an Eastern mountain gorilla. This species is very bright and has human-like qualities. Tank comes from the Volcanoes National Park in the Albertine Mountain Range of Rwanda."

"Boy, you really know a lot about Tank's family tree and where he comes from," his partner in the booth said to him.

The announcer nodded in the affirmative, before adding, "I just thought our viewing audience would like to know about the person throwing a perfect spiral pass more than 100 yards."

With that said, the show ended. However, the announcer reminded his viewing audience, "Tank was found in his dead mother's arms, with his innards being eaten by a hyena. He was the only surviving member of his troop—his gorilla family—of 26.

"The rescuers didn't believe he'd survive the trip from the jungle to the park hospital. He did, and they rushed him into surgery, again not believing he'd survive. But he did.

"It was touch and go for weeks and months. However, Tank was a fighter. After all he had gone through, he wasn't about to give up. With the help of his brothers' closeness and smells, Tank believed he was just one of the brothers, and with that thought, he began eating more, and that made him stronger. In a few months' time, he was crawling with the best of them.

"Tank and his brothers were about the same age when he was found—two months old. They banded together, and that's when the Boyagians—who are veterinarians—decided to keep Tank in the family. They adopted him and, soon after, brought him back to the States. That is the life story of Tank, the mountain gorilla and Sports Phenom!"

"Thank you for that," his partner said, adding, "It was quite a history lesson for our viewers. I'm sure they learned a lot about Tank."

***

Tank had thought that was the end of it. He refused to be the center of attention. That was getting old.

But, oh no! The local and international media got caught up in Tank's incredible life story.

After the game, the boys and Tank returned to their dorm room to celebrate the win. There was a frat party at the frat house, but the brothers and Tank were no shows.

For some reason, one camera crew continued to follow Tank wherever he went on campus. Tank didn't care for that at all!

After a while, Jerome phoned the university police and had the camera crew escorted off the property and banned for life, never to be allowed on university property again. If they dared to return and were caught, prison time was a given.

***

The time came for Tank to return to Los Angeles. As Hazel waited in her car, the brothers and Tank hugged and said their goodbyes.

Less than an hour later, Tank was home. Traffic had been so light that the trip had taken almost an hour less than usual.

Back at school, the principal had kept his word and had promoted Tank to the twelfth grade.

Chapter 11

The year went by pretty fast. Now constantly in the news, Tank was bombarded by communications from colleges and universities in the United States and the rest of the world. They all wanted Tank on their football, basketball, and hockey teams. Even his brothers hoped to add Tank to their football team.

Schools' athletic directors now offered Tank the world—anything he wanted—to play for their teams. As always, however, all those schools lacked one important thing—Tank's brothers. Tank would only play for a team that included his brothers.

Tank was a walk-on for his brothers' football team. Their wish was fulfilled. His brothers were all very tall— the shortest was 6'7" and the tallest was 6'9". Tank, when standing upright, was nearly eight feet tall, and with his arms stretched upward while standing, he was nearly eleven feet tall. He was the perfect height to stand underneath the basket and, with ball in hand, dunk it without leaving the floor, just as he'd done when he was in middle school.

The many schools that had football and basketball teams weren't very happy hearing that Tank was now a member of both the football and basketball teams of the UCLA Bruins. With a little research, they discovered the case that had been brought against Tank by five elementary schools and how they'd got him banned from the game. The college teams thought they might be able to do the same.

Knowing this, both the LA football and basketball teams used Tank sparingly, only playing him when the team was losing by a large amount or winning by double digits. They hoped the other schools would forget about suing. It would pay off if they did, because Tank brought in money from both sides of the aisle, win or lose.

***

Tank was right! He was a sideshow but a profitable one. He filled the stadiums wherever they played and brought hundreds of thousands of dollars to the teams and neighborhood bars and restaurants.

Tank was good for the teams' pocketbooks. Simple as that. Without him in the game, the stadiums were half-filled, and the loss in dollars was substantial and noticeable.

Tank was still the talk of the town, and NFL commissioner Roger Goodell hadn't forgotten the day that the three sports agents had come to visit and talk with him—the subject being Tank.

Goodell had a meeting with all the owners of the leagues to give him the go-ahead to add a bylaw to the NFL's rulebook to allow Tank to enter the draft—but only if he could pass a few strenuous tests. If he passed, Tank would be allowed in the draft for rookies. If he failed, he could try the UFL or the USFL.

***

The tests were given, and Tank passed with flying colors! He was now possible NFL material.

As the news materialized concerning Tank and the NFL draft, his name was on the tip of everybody's tongues but only if they were interested in football. Once again, Tank was the talk of the town.

The news media in the US and around the world were interested in Tank's story, and many put Tank's photo on their front pages. Under their headlines, they would mention Tank for one reason or another. Most mentioned his football prowess and his mammoth size. He now weighed nearly 500 pounds, and when sitting, his body was so large that it completely covered a hockey net. Nobody could get a puck past him.

Tank dominated hockey, football, and basketball. He was a billion dollar asset to any sports team. And now that Commissioner Roger Goodell of the NFL considered Tank to be "human," he was definitely the number one pick. However, the team that would get that number one pick hadn't been decided yet.

Everyone in the US and around the world watched to see who would win the number one draft pick. Others from around the world were also watching the news, but only when Tank was the story.

***

With Tank in the public eye once again, the Asian gangs remembered when their comrades in arms had been caught by the FBI more than 10 years ago and had been run out of the country and promised prison time if they ever returned to the United States. These weren't the same gangsters who had wanted to kidnap Tank ten years ago, but others were now considering going to America to kidnap Tank and take him back to their homelands to be auctioned off over the internet to tight-knit billionaire clients. Many of those clients were considered very "odd" because of their fetish for monkey brain consumption.

The first gang that had tried to kidnap Tank more than 10 years ago had experienced a fiasco. The new gangs, however, were sure that could never happen again and had their caper all planned out.

Eight gang members from Indonesia arrived without any problems with customs and with no Feds on their tails. So far, so good. They moved into a motel near their mark and rented a panel van with sliding side doors that was perfect for a kidnapping.

They planned to kidnap and then drug Tank with a heavy narcotic that would knock him out almost immediately. They would then stuff him in a large wooden box that would have holes drilled in all sides to let oxygen in so that Tank could breathe. He would then be driven across the border into Mexico, where a charter aircraft would be waiting to take Tank on a 26 hour trip to Indonesia in the cargo hold.

Jakarta, Indonesia, was where the auction would take place. The opening bid would be set at 4 million US dollars and was expected to go as high as 25 million.

The sale would include a live video feed over the internet, beginning the moment the top of the ape's skull was cut away to the main course—the eating of said brain—and continuing until the very moment the ape succumbed to death.

Those clients who tried to purchase said ape but lost the bidding war would have the chance—for a "nominal" fee of just 100,000 US dollars—to watch the extraordinary event on live TV. That amount of money was "loose change" to those billionaires.

With tens of millions of dollars at stake, there was no going back for the gangsters. They were all in, which meant they would kidnap Tank or die trying. And they were aware that Tank no longer had his 12-man security team protecting him.

For a decade, Tank had stayed out of the limelight, but now another 100-yard pass brought him back into it. And with no security detail protecting him and with his brothers away at college, Tank's only protection now was Hazel, the nanny. And she was one tough cookie.

Tank wasn't worried. He had no security, but he was constantly surrounded by sports agents and other bloodsucking representatives from the many companies who wanted Tank on their boards of directors. He was a feather in any company's hat, if they had Tank on their side.

Others who kept harassing Tank were NFL personnel, who took measurements for his uniforms. They found that his size was a new record for NFL players. His jersey measured six times larger than that of any other player in the history of the NFL, measuring to an XXXXXXXXXXXL (extra-large times ten). The record before that was XXXXXL. He also set a record for both weight and height. Tank was 112 pounds heavier than any current or past recorded professional football player—the record was 390 pounds. He was also seven inches taller than any football player, past or present, standing at seven feet ten inches. His shoes were size 34 with an eight inch width.

Tank's size was mammoth, but he proved that he was an excellent player in nearly all sports. He was an all-around jock and was sure to be the number one pick in the NFL draft!

The team that would get to pick number one still wasn't confirmed yet, and the owners were getting a little anxious waiting for Goodell and team to decide that outcome.

No matter which team was able to pick Tank, Goodell was sure to get some blowback from teams that couldn't select him for their teams. They couldn't file suit in court against an "ape" playing in the NFL, as that had already been decided by the meeting Goodell had with all the owners concerning Tank being allowed to play in the NFL. They had all agreed on the new bylaw amendment that had been added to the NFL rulebook and constitution, so those issues had been decided and nothing and no one could change them.

When Goodell's team finally decided who would get the first round draft pick, it went to the Tennessee Titans. The Titans made it known that Tank would be their pick for number one.

***

But the gang members from Indonesia had different plans. The NFL draft was not on their minds—only that

Tank would be number one in their draft and be taken for a 25 million dollar payoff!

For three nights before the NFL draft was to take place, four of the eight Indonesian gangsters had followed Tank and his nanny, waiting for their opening to pounce!

Usually, after the nanny had picked Tank up from school, they would drive directly to the zoo so Tank could teach his students—all 44 of them. However, on this particular afternoon, they first went to Griffith Park to eat and wash down a few morsels of food before going to the zoo, which was on the park grounds.

As they were getting ready to head for the zoo, a man came out of nowhere and asked Tank if he had seen a small kitten. He explained that the kitten was a gift for his daughter. Hazel was busy cleaning up the picnic table, so Tank walked with the man toward a white panel van with an open sliding door.

Tank saw the kitten near the van. Excited, he ran up to it and picked it up. He was about to put the kitten into the van through the open door when he felt three small pricks to his hairy skin. He did not know that they were tranquilizers fired from a tranquilizer gun by the man who had befriended him.

***

Hazel saw what was happening to Tank. In shock, she began screaming as loud as she could, but the park was empty at that time of day, and nobody heard her.

Tank tried to put up a fight, but the drugs injected into his bloodstream made him too sleepy. He was shoved into the van, and within seconds, the van, the gangsters and Tank were heading into the wild blue yonder.

Hazel jumped into her car. She managed to catch up with the van and followed behind it. She saw that they were headed to the airport.

***

The ride to the airport went as the Indonesians had planned. Now they had to figure out a way to lift Tank into the ventilated wooden box they had built a few days before.

They pulled the box out of the van and placed it on the ground next to the van's sliding door. To their dismay, the box was two feet higher than the floor of the van. Even if they could somehow lift Tank into the box, they could not see how they were going to get it into the cargo hold of the charter flight that was waiting on the tarmac for them. They had no equipment to lift the box with Tank in it onto the plane. Nevertheless, they at least tried to get Tank out of the van and into the box.

"Come on you guys, lift!" yelled one gangster to the others. But Tank was too pliable, too "loosey, goosey," too "roly-poly." To put it mildly, he was just too heavy.

"Are we stupid or what," another wondered out loud.

"Man, I thought we had this all planned out," said another to his gangster friends.

The gangsters realized things weren't going too good for them, and they began yelling at one another. Their voices increased in volume and were soon loud enough that a security guard making his rounds heard the commotion and wandered over to check it out.

"You guys need some help?" he called out as he approached the van.

"No, we're okay," they replied.

But things didn't look quite right to the guard, so he called for backup—just in case the men tried something unexpected.

He walked toward them. When he got within 15 feet of the van, he could see a hairy mass of body and hair in the open side doorway. As he drew nearer, he noticed that that the mass of body and hair was actually a real live gorilla, an endangered species. *These men must be trying to smuggle it out of the country,* he thought.

He pulled his gun from its holster and held the men at bay. "You guys sit down on the ground, and we'll wait until backup arrives," said the guard.

Within minutes, his backup arrived, with Hazel in third place. And the Boyagians were a distant fourth.

The backup cops began handcuffing the men, determined to detain the Indonesians until they explained why a drugged gorilla was in their midst!

The detained men tried to bribe the officers and guard. "We'll give you 20,000 US dollars, all cash, if you let us go," said a dejected handcuffed gangster.

But the officers of the law were honest men and refused 20,000 US dollars cash to allow the men to flee.

"Are you guys stupid or what," said one of the cops laughing. "Trying to lift a five-hundred-pound gorilla without a hoist."

A second police car showed up, and the cops placed all four men into the back of their cruisers. The gangsters' plan to kidnap Tank and take him back to their homeland was completely foiled by the quick action of the security guard and the LAPD.

***

The Boyagians, after showing their identification and explaining to the policemen that Tank was their adopted son, were finally allowed to see him. Reaching into her doctor's bag, Mariam found an antidote to the drug Tank had been given.

In less than a minute after receiving the antidote, Tank was sitting up and seemed to be okay. Just in case, though, he was taken to the Boyagian Veterinary Hospital for observation.

So Tank was headed to the hospital, and his kidnappers were headed to jail for a long, long time. As Tank put it, "They are menace to society."

***

However, Tank wasn't out of the woods yet. He and the Boyagians were unaware that eight gangsters had been sent from Jakarta to America as part of an eight-man crew. Only four of them were now in jail. The other four were awaiting their instructions to complete their task as planned.

The cops were also unaware of the threat still looming against Tank! Unless the cops could get confessions from the four gangsters now headed to jail, Tank would be a sitting duck, unaware that four other gangsters still lurked in the shadows, waiting to kidnap him and fly him back to Jakarta.

Nobody but the gangsters knew when and where they would attack Tank next.

Chapter 12

Believing that his troubles were behind him, Tank went about his day without a care in the world. He was anxious to return to the zoo to teach his students, and now he decided he would also try to teach them football, which would be much harder to learn than sign language.

At the end of the week, his plan was to have Hazel drive him to the university to watch the Thanksgiving Day parade and then his brothers' Thanksgiving Day football game. This game was very important. If the brothers' team won, they would get to play a Bowl game! So, a lot was riding on the upcoming game.

Even more importantly, the NFL draft was slowly approaching and would be televised. A camera crew was to be stationed in Tank's brothers' dorm room to get their reactions to Tank being drafted in the first round. Tank and his parents would be at the studio.

The sports aficionados had all picked Tank as their number one draft pick. The Tennessee Titans' front office unofficially stated that Tank would be their pick. However, they didn't know for sure that they had the first pick until Commissioner Goodell went in front of the cameras.

"The Tennessee Titans have won the first pick in the first round of the NFL's draft pick," MC Roger Goodell declared. "And they have picked Tank Boyagian for their first round pick in the NFL's 2025 football draft!" he added, barely containing his excitement.

Half the crowd hooted and hollered excitedly, but the other half sat on their hands in silence, mesmerized by the thought that the first draft pick in the NFL's 2025 football draft was an ape or mountain gorilla—an endangered species. They didn't know what to make of a gorilla playing professional football. They were certain that he could play, as many in the crowd had seen videos of Tank playing football years before with his brothers. Yeah, he could play . . . but they were certain that he'd be a major distraction and hindrance to the game, rather than a benefit.

Only time would tell if fame and fortune would grace the Titans and, with any luck, trickle down to the other teams and the league. If that happened, then all would prosper. Perhaps, one day, the league would allow other apes to play in the game or in the sports arena.

Just then, two big men walked across the stage. Each held onto an arm of Tank's jersey, and spread it out tight across the stage. Four large men, each weighing approximately 200 pounds apiece, stood next to each other in a row in front of the jersey. The men were still smaller than the jersey.

Tank's jersey was nearly seven feet across. It was gigantic next to others, and that was how big Tank was compared to the average lineman. If he fell on top of one of them, he could kill them, either by suffocation or by breaking bones.

It was hard to imagine having to go against a player like Tank—someone who was four or five times a typical player in size and weight and much taller in height. That was a losing proposition—guaranteed. The question wasn't whether Tank could hold his own when playing professional football, but how many opponents would he put into the hospital?

Most of the crowd were still hooting and hollering. Tank noticed them and followed their lead. He didn't know why, but he began clapping too. He looked around, bewildered and wondering what all the fuss was about. Just then, his parents came on stage to congratulate and hug their son. Tank's father's height was a good six feet seven inches (6'7") tall and weighed nearly 300 pounds but standing alongside Tank, his father looked quite small.

The men handed Tank the jersey so he could hold it up to show the crowd. He did, and that act showed just how enormous Tank was. He wasn't just huge or large, he was mammoth, gigantic. No other words could describe him. He looked like an adult and other players looked like kids next to him. His body was immense.

His parents were so proud of him and his accomplishments. The MC proudly read off the list of Tank's accomplishments—from living and pulling through surgery on that fateful day in Rwanda to teaching other apes to sign. The MC noted that Tank's students were fast learners and even better students than human ones.

He also mentioned how Tank's students were wanting to learn and sat in one group without disrupting his class for bathroom breaks. None of his students fidgeted in their seats, nor were they bored or not wanting to learn.

Goodell then mentioned Tank's brothers and wanted to get their reactions to Tank being the number one pick in the 2025 draft. All five brothers were suddenly on television.

"Yeah, we're proud of him," said Jerome. The brothers gave each other high-fives, smiling from ear to ear as they celebrated Tank's incredible win and his journey from baby to present day.

"It was an incredible journey," Broadway Joe told the viewing audience. "And now, Tank's going to do great things in the NFL. He won't be stopped."

The reporter then asked the brothers, "Have any of you been asked to play on the team so you can sign the play to Tank?"

"No," replied Walter. "Tank can understand the English language. He only signs when he's talking to my mother or his class. He understands a few of the standard running plays, and when he's playing defense, he doesn't have to see the ball because he can smell it. He can smell the pigskin, and his nose takes him directly to the ball. He reacts and tackles the opponent. Simple as that." Walter then added, "Tank will break every record in the record books. That's all I've got to say." He looked directly into the camera and exclaimed, "Go get 'em, Tank!"

Tank's brothers didn't need to be on the team to help him. Tank could understand English, and if he needed to ask any questions, the Titans had a player on the team who could communicate using sign language. The player had been born deaf, but had inner ear implants inserted as a young adult and could now hear. Furthermore, Hazel usually stayed with Tank on the road, and at home always watching from the sidelines. So Tank had no problems learning the plays.

***

The coach also believed Tank would do great things on the football field. And Tank didn't disappoint. In his first NFL game, he had six quarterback sacks before the first half and stopped four different runs that would have been touchdowns had not Tank stopped them with crushing blows. He also blocked three field goals and created and recovered four fumbles.

That was his play on defense. On offense, he scored six touchdowns for 330 yards, scored six two-point conversions, and ran cover for three other offensive touchdowns. Tank was responsible for 48 of the final 69 points in just his first game playing as a Tennessee Titan.

Tank was finally benched near the end of the third quarter. The Titans were so far ahead that their opponents could never catch up with the time remaining. So, the Titan coach decided to replace Tank with a substitute who would take Tank's place on the field, not in play-making but in spirit only. No one could really take Tank's place.

Tank was definitely the hero and MVP in his first game played. He had no trouble listening to and understanding the coach or running the plays. He understood the plays verbally, with no trouble.

Tank continued his progress, playing both offense and defense. He needed only three quarters to put the game so far out of reach for the opposing team that he sat out for the rest of the games, always nearing the end of the third quarter when a substitute was always inserted in his place.

Once Tank was off the field and not making plays any more, the opposing teams always began scoring. Tank's coach allowed this, as it made the score appear less lopsided. This was done to appease the opposing coaches and teams.

By the fifth game, Tank's coach was hearing complaints from the opposing coaches that playing Tank was unfair to the opposing teams, as they couldn't stop him when running the ball for the offense and couldn't get the opposing team players past him.

Teams began filing complaints with Commissioner Roger Goodell concerning Tank and his team's unfair advantage when Tank was playing. They wanted Tank banned from professional football, even though he was bringing in tens of millions of dollars to the league and to the teams the Titans played against.

This wasn't their only complaint. Tank was putting opposing players in the hospital on an average of three per game. When he tackled them and fell on top of them, he crushed their innards and chests. That put the players on the injured list, and many were out for the season, unable to return to play.

The opposing teams whined to the commissioner, but he basically told them, "Quit your whining! Tank's good for business and the bottom line of every team in the league. So, get on board, or forfeit your games if you don't want to play against Tank. Right now, he's football. The fans love him, especially the kids. We get hundreds of fan mail letters for Tank every day saying how they love him and how great he's made the game of football. And the ratings when he's playing have gone through the roof. They are up 40 points when he plays. So, love it or leave it! Get me!"

With that said, the coaches were shown the door. Goodell didn't want to be bothered by them when Tank was putting tens of millions of dollars in their coffers every week. This was a no-brainer! Tank was good for business, pure and simple.

***

After playing in just eight games, Tank really had earned his pay for a rookie. He led the league in nearly every category, breaking record after record for most touchdowns on kickoffs—9 and most consecutive touchdowns on kickoffs—8; most touchdowns for running back—18; most fumbles created—10; most fumbles recovered—8; most recovered fumbles for touchdowns—8; most fumbles recovered for touchdown—8; most quarterback sacks—24; most passes knocked down at line of scrimmage—28; most blocked field goals—6; and last but not least, most opposing players put in hospital—22.

It took Tank to do in eight games what Hall of Famers couldn't do in a season. He was the envy of all the players, both defensive and offensive. They wished they had one-tenth the abilities Tank had. He was unstoppable!

However, Tank was becoming a thorn in Goodell's side. The opposing coaches' rumbling and whining was getting louder and louder. They were making their arguments and opinions known. They wanted Tank gone at any cost, even at the cost of losing tens of millions of dollars that Tank brought to each team and the league. Most were of the same opinion—Tank was just too *good* to play in the NFL. None of the other great players could compete with Tank. And with each future game, those records would be broken again and again.

Goodell met with the owners and gave them their coaches' reasons for ridding the game of Tank. And it boiled down to one main reason—Tank was just too good for the game. He made great players look bad as he made 67 percent of the plays both offensively and defensively.

After listening to the coaches' arguments and reasoning, all the owners but one relented. The Titan's owner refused to go along with banning Tank from the game.

Goodell was crushed. He had thought that the owners would never bend, not wanting to lose the Golden Goose. Goodell was left with no choice. But he didn't ban Tank; instead, he only suspended him for the rest of the season—a total of nine games not including playoff games. He hoped the owners would come to their senses and once again bring Tank to the game of professional football.

Tank was saddened, especially because he was given no reason for the suspension. He thought he had done something wrong. His Union representatives and Tank's agent questioned the move and expected heavy fines for the owners. However, Tank decided he would return to the classroom to teach his pupils at the zoo.

When word leaked out about Tank's suspension, his agent met with the Boyagians to request their permission to shop Tank to the National Hockey League. His phone had been ringing off the hook from the general managers of more than a dozen NHL hockey teams. He believed he could swing a contract for Tank as a goalie.

The general managers had been interested in Tank over a year ago, just before he was drafted by the Titans, but they hadn't acted fast enough. Now was their chance, and they didn't want to miss out on it.

Tank's agent was able to get him tryouts with a dozen NHL teams in front of their general managers and more were calling daily to get Tank's attention.

Over the next two weeks, Tank tried out for a dozen different NHL teams. The players shot puck after puck at 120 miles per hour, trying their best to get one into the net and past Tank. They couldn't do it. Tank was so huge that he covered the net completely, with no room to fit a puck.

After trying out for those teams, Tank picked his and his family's favorite—the LA Kings. The Los Angeles hockey team was close to home, so when his brothers were home, they could come and see him play.

His coach's instructions were simple. "Don't let the puck get into the net. Stop them at all costs."

On the road and at home, Tank's nanny Hazel again agreed to travel with him for hockey season, just as she had for the football season.

Chapter 13

Tank was full of nerves before the Opening Day hockey game. But when the game began, his nerves suddenly disappeared, especially after he swatted away the first puck shot at him.

The hockey game went the same as the football games Tank had played in. He couldn't be stopped. Not one puck from the opposing players made it into the net. They even tried getting the rebounds of pucks that bounced off Tank's chest protector if they landed close to the net, but they couldn't even push those pucks past Tank.

Tank kicked, swatted, and threw shots away like he was throwing peanuts to the zoo animals, and the opposing team could do nothing. It seemed like Tank was larger than the net. The opposing players thought so, anyway.

Meanwhile, the Kings worked their magic and worked their opponent's goalie pretty hard, scoring six goals for the win, 6–0.

The Standing Room Only crowd clapped, hooted, hollered, and howled with excitement and happiness over the win, and especially for their favorite rookie.

Tank's teammates surrounded him and congratulated him. They tried lifting him onto their shoulders but quickly gave up. Trying to lift a gorilla with his goalie equipment on was difficult, to say the least.

A mountain gorilla his age (Tank was now nearly 20) should weigh from 350 to upward of 400 pounds, but Tank, who was still a growing boy, weighed in at around 500 pounds. But no matter. His swift moves and strength that had helped him when playing football was now helping him play the game of professional hockey.

The NHL owners had to admit that Tank brought people into the seats. Some nights in the past, the Kings couldn't give seats away. Now, Tank played to Standing Room Only. The arena was packed to the rafters.

While the football ratings were plummeting downward, hockey's TV ratings were going sky high, all due to Tank's arrival at the NHL! And the sponsors and investors threw money at the owners, wanting to be part of the phenomenon named Tank Boyagian.

Again, the news media blew up the story. Headlines for the LA Times read: Phenom gorilla stops Red Wings 6-0 to SRO crowd. Below the headlines was a photo of the Kings' new goalie—Tank Boyagian, in all his protective gear. His teammates called him TB for short!

Tank quickly became part of the team. His teammates took him to different tourist places when on the road and even to some bars to show him off to their fans. But when they put a beer in front of him, he pushed it to the side, signing the words for "bad water" and refused to drink it. He still remembered the results from the frat party. So, other than that, Tank was happy to get the attention. He was now one of the boys.

***

Tank's next 20 games went the same as the first. And during the first two periods of Tank's next game, the opposing players couldn't score on 46 shots. In the third period, they gave up completely trying to get the puck past Tank. They just couldn't do it.

On this night, the Kings only needed one goal for the win against the Boston Bruins, 1–0.

As the game ended and the opponents headed to their clubhouse, they could be heard swearing and complaining and just carrying on to their coaches. One said, "It does no good to try and score."

Another said, "We can't get it past that goalie!"

"You gotta get rid of him, Coach!" said another.

"But he makes lots of money for the owners," the coach replied. "It would be a hard sell! If I can't say something against that goalie who fills the stadium with fans that neither us nor the Kings could fill. It's that goalie that puts butts in the seats! That means mega-dollars for the owners. For now, we're just gonna have to suck it up and live with it. And anyway, the Kings' owner wouldn't go for it since they've only lost one game and that was when they rested Tank and didn't play him. Be thankful we only have to play the Kings a few times a year, and they aren't even in our conference. But, I'll speak to the GM about your concerns. Go ahead and shower, guys."

At every game, Tank shut out the opposing teams, and the grumbling continued getting louder and louder. Finally, it reached the teams' owners.

The coaches in both conferences that had played the Kings were grumbling the loudest because they just couldn't score a goal. Tank shut them out, not allowing any team to score when he was in goal. The only time the Kings lost was when Tank sat out of the game and his substitute played. Tank, in games played, was 32 and 0. So far, so good. Or so he thought.

***

Tank was happy playing hockey. He was one of the boys. But he was happiest when his brothers returned home from college so the family could be together once again. They smothered each other with hugs, kisses, and love. They acted like little kids again, wrestling and rolling around on the floor. He was ever so happy.

The Kings had a game on Easter Sunday after the Easter parade and Tank invited his parents and five brothers to the game as his guest.

They loved watching their brother and son play professional hockey, just as they had loved watching Tank play professional football. He was great at anything he tried, especially sports. It came so easily to him. He would watch others play a game, and he would pick it up within minutes and soon be outplaying the others. It just came naturally to Tank.

After the game, while he was speaking with his family, a great sports player came up and introduced himself to Tank and his family. The great sports player was none other than Mike Trout, right fielder for the Los Angeles Angels. He invited Tank and family to be his guests at Anaheim Stadium in two days' time for Opening Day.

The brothers had to decline the offer because they had to get back to classes. Tank accepted the offer, although saddened that his brothers couldn't come with him, but he understood.

That morning, Mike Trout sent the Angels limousine for Tank. Tank's brothers were leaving for college. Before going, they gave hugs and kisses to their hairy brother. Tank would be visiting with them sooner rather than later. They walked Tank to the limousine for his day at the Park, with Hazel following close behind. Tank and Hazel got into the car, and Tank waved goodbye to his brothers. They waved back as they got into their car and drove away.

Twenty minutes later, Tank and Hazel were at the ballpark and Mike Trout was there to meet them. All his teammates had also gathered to meet the great "sports phenom." They'd seen Tank play NFL football and now watched him play NHL hockey. They agreed that Tank had the best winning streak of both NHL conferences, with 38 wins and no losses.

The group walked into the Angels clubhouse, where they surprised Tank with a special gift—his own Angels' uniform complete with jersey, pants, belt, socks, and hat. Everything but shoes. Two players held out the jersey like others had done during his draft pick night for football. When stretched out, the jersey was four feet wide. Four good-sized people standing next to each other in a row could fit into it. That's how wide the jersey was. There was laughter in the clubhouse as they helped Tank put on his jersey. Trout then placed the Angels hat on Tank's head, and they all accompanied Trout through the dugout and onto the field.

Tank stopped for a minute and took in the beautiful scenery, especially the lush green grass. He bent down and grabbed a handful of it, holding it up to his nose and smelling it. Then he began eating it, signing the word "good," which Hazel interpreted for the players.

Trout and his buddies laughed at Tank's words. "I'm glad you like it, Tank!" Trout replied. "Help yourself."

They all walked over to the batter's box and let Tank watch as they tried to hit the ball. Trout noticed that Tank was mesmerized as he watched the batter hit the ball. Tank seemed puzzled that no one could hit it out of the infield.

Another batter had stepped into the batting cage and stood at the plate, waiting for his pitch from his teammate. But the pitcher wasn't ready, so the batter bent down, grabbed a handful of dirt, rubbed it in his hands, and then tossed it aside.

Tank watched as the batter took a few practice swings before the ball reached the plate. The batter swung and missed the first pitch, swinging at air. The next pitch fared no better. He missed again.

Tank now seemed to be salivating at the mouth, clearly wanting to try his hand at hitting the ball. He had played ball with his brothers almost as much as he'd played football.

Tank spoke in sign to Trout. Hazel gladly interpreted. "Tank, hit ball."

Trout grabbed the biggest bat he could find close by and handed it to Tank. The bat looked like a mini-bat in Tank's hands—the kind one could buy at the stadium from a vendor for five bucks.

All the players, including the opposing team, gathered round the cage to watch Tank.

Tank mimicked the last batter by bending down, grabbing a handful of dirt, rubbing it between his hands, and then throwing it down on the ground. He then stood at the plate in the batter's box, anxiously awaiting the pitch.

The pitcher was playing no favorites. He wasn't going to pitch to Tank any differently than he had to the other players. He wanted to see if Tank was as good at baseball as he was at football and hockey.

The first pitch was a slow curve. Tank swung hard, wanting to hit the ball over the fences, but he only got air. He missed badly. The players watching wanted to laugh, but Tank was their guest, so they kept their laughing muffled.

Tank missed the next pitch, again only getting air. The third pitch he made contact with the ball, but at the end of the bat, and fouled it off. The next pitch was a 98 mph fastball, but Tank saw the ball and hit it.

The players were flabbergasted that he'd even hit the ball. Tank hit it so hard that it flew out fast and up, farther and farther, nearly out of the stadium. The ball landed 480 feet into the left field stands.

The players couldn't believe it. They figured Tank had just got lucky; that the home run ball was just a fluke.

The pitcher threw another fastball across the plate near the 100 mph mark. Tank again clobbered the ball. This time, it sailed over the centerfield wall and well over the rock formation and fountain.

Ball after pitched ball, Tank hit with power. The next dozen or so pitches all went far over all three walls. Those watching couldn't believe their eyes. What Tank was doing was amazing.

He could easily become the DH for the Angels. They really needed another power hitter. After watching Tank hit the ball with so much power, they thought of him as a Babe Ruth, or Hank Aaron. Tank was a fantastic hitter.

They wanted to watch him throw the ball, too, but he had no glove to fit his hands, having left his custom-made glove back at his house. However, he did throw the ball from home plate to the centerfield wall 400 feet away with very little effort.

The players from both teams were in awe of Tank and couldn't believe what they had just witnessed. The guy was truly a "sports phenom!"

The game was about to start, so Hazel and Tank sat in their guest seats next to the dugout and watched the Angels beat the Red Sox 7–1.

Trout and the others said their goodbyes, wishing Tank well and telling him that when he tired of hockey, they could use him on their team.

Tank and Hazel rode the limousine back to their home. Once inside, Tank couldn't quit talking about his day at the ballpark. He was as giddy as a school kid. He went to his room, found his baseball mitt, put it on his hand, and didn't remove it until he went to bed.

He thanked Hazel for accompanying him to the ball game. He signed to her, "much fun."

***

While Tank was having fun playing baseball, the powers that be were grumbling once again. The complaints were coming from more than just the NHL coaches. Now, hotel managers didn't want Tank to stay in their hotels.

One hotel manager told the coach, "If you bring Tank here to stay, then no one associated with your team is wanted. We'll refuse the team hospitality and rooms." The manager's reasoning was that the feeding needs of a gorilla were a problem, as finding the roots, bushes, and flowers for Tank was much too difficult, although the fruit was no problem.

The Kings owner also began to grumble, as he was now hearing the woes concerning Tank's food regimen. He had to make special arrangements so Tank could stay with his teammates. He promised the hotels that the Kings would find the food Tank needed and that ended the hotels' refusal to house the team. The managers now had no problem with Tank staying at their hotels if they didn't have to find the food to feed him. He was a hard one to satisfy.

The team's "gopher" was given the task of finding the food that Tank needed to keep him healthy. In each city they traveled to, he had to ask the city's zoo for the food needed to satisfy Tank's hunger.

Tank was still undefeated as goalie, and the grumbling from team owners and coaches that wanted Tank gone from the NHL was getting louder. Just like the NFL had done, the NHL coaches now started saying, "Tank is just too good for this sport."

However, getting rid of Tank from the NHL would be hard, as Commissioner Goodell of the NFL had discovered. Tank was in the sports news section of the LA Times and other local papers nearly every day, and the writers were always talking up Tank's skill, agility, and quickness. And his ability to stop the other teams from scoring.

When Tank was in goal, the opposing teams had never scored a goal. All the kids loved him, as he would sign autographs, using his handprint as his signature. The kids couldn't get enough of Tank. They were his biggest fans and had their parents buy wall posters of Tank with and without his hockey garb. When Tank played, the ratings went up 40 percent and increased even more when the team played in their home arena.

The owners had their work cut out for them if they wanted to rid the NHL of Tank. Commissioner Gary Bettman wouldn't have it as easy as Commissioner Goodell had. No matter.

But the grumbling continued among opposing NHL coaches, their players, and the owners. The King's owner wasn't having any of it and threatened to sue if they suspended Tank for no reason other than that he was "too good for the sport." That didn't sit too well with him, and he actually felt sick even thinking about getting rid of Tank. The Kings were leading the league in wins and points only because of Tank. Now, the other owners wanted Tank out of the game completely.

Chapter 14

The Kings were playing in a playoff game in the third week in May. Back in Indonesia, the four remaining gangsters saw Tank on Los Angeles TV. They realized that Tank would most likely be staying at his parents' house in Los Angeles . . .

***

Tank's brothers were also visiting at home, since they had finished their semester. A second family reunion was happening, with everyone together again. Tank was so happy being with his parents and brothers.

As Tank and his brothers wrestled together on the floor, an announcer interrupted the show and told the viewing audience that the Kings' goalie, Tank Boyagian, had been suspended from the NHL. No reason was given.

The NHL had not even had the guts to tell Tank in person about the suspension. It was truly shameful. Commissioner Bettman was no better than Commissioner Goodell.

However, Bettman would soon regret his actions. The fans were in an uproar over this decision and couldn't understand it, especially as the NHL was giving no reason. The Kings front office promised an update very soon.

***

Just hours after the announcement of Tank's suspension from the NHL, the general managers of the LA Lakers basketball team and the Los Angeles Angels baseball team began competing for Tank's signature on a contract. The Lakers wanted him as a starting center with LeBron. The Angels wanted him as their designated hitter. No minor league play. They'd start him in the majors.

Trout said of Tank, "If he can hit the ball like he did the day he took batting practice, then we've got ourselves a keeper."

After getting the okay from the Boyagians, Tank's agent set up a time for tryouts for both teams.

Tank played both sports well. In basketball, he could dunk the ball without leaving the floor. And he could run faster than his teammates from one end of the floor to the other. Using his long arms and reach, he could block passes and he had a great sky hook. And he could dribble the ball with the best of them. Tank was an amazing basketball player. His play could turn any team around into a winning team.

When playing basketball in eighth grade for Adams Junior High, Tank had broken the state record by scoring

122 points. The opponents scored just four points. To say the least, that was a lopsided basketball score.

***

The day Tank tried out for the Angels (this time, he brought his glove), they had their best fastball pitcher try to strike Tank out. The pitcher had a 100 mph fastball with a four inch up and down movement.

Tank grabbed the bat Trout handed to him and stepped into the batter's box. He was dressed in the Angels uniform that Trout and the team had given him. He bent down, grabbed a handful of dirt, smelled it, rubbed it between his hands, and then threw it back down onto the ground. He shuffled his feet, trying to get comfortable at the plate and in a good stance before trying to hit the ball. Now he was ready.

The other players not in the field gathered around the batting cage to watch whether Tank could do what he had done before—hit the long ball.

Tank only batted right-handed. His brothers had tried teaching him to hit as a switch-hitter, but Tank wasn't successful hitting left-handed.

The pitcher threw his first pitch—a fastball, outside and low. Tank was smart and had a good eye, so he didn't chase the pitch. He refused to swing at any pitch outside his comfort zone. The next pitch was waist high, right down the middle of the plate, and clocking at 102 mph.

124

But this pitch didn't have a chance of making it past Tank. He hit the ball with such power and velocity that it was over the left field fence in less than two seconds. It landed in the seats 40 rows deep, nearly 410 feet from home plate.

Tank crushed the ball in the next ten pitches. All hits reached beyond the fences, so the manager decided to bring in a hard-throwing left-handed submariner who threw from an underhand or sidearm position that gave the ball a sinking effect. That pitcher had four main pitches—a 96 to 98 mph two-seam fastball (sometimes called a two-finger fastball), a four-finger fastball with a pop, a slider, and a slow curveball.

Tank stepped out of the batter's box to adjust his helmet. He signed a comment to Trout, which Hazel interpreted, "Too easy, pitcher." And Tank added a kind of laughing sound.

Tank was right. He hit all four of the pitcher's pitches past the fences, no less than 440 feet.

The team's manager and general manager had seen enough to know they wanted Tank on their team, ASAP. They had witnessed a real "Sports Phenom." Tank was the real deal.

The Angels front office believed they had the best shot at signing Tank to a multi-year contract for approximately 800 million dollars for ten years.

Tank was young and in great health, with outstanding baseball abilities. He had at least a 15 to 20-year baseball career ahead of him, if he wanted it. And there would be no reason to suspend him, because he was too good. They wanted Tank as their DH for as long as Tank wanted to play. They knew he'd be a great player, another Babe Ruth, Mickey Mantle, or Hank Aaron, and Tank didn't smoke or drink.

***

The Lakers believed Tank would be a great addition to their team. LeBron James wanted him as a teammate, and so did LeBron's grandkids. The Lakers wanted to sign Tank to a long-term contract to play center for their team. They had to get the fans back, and Tank would do that. Tank was like a big little kid. Either team would be lucky to get him.

Tank's agent was given an amount of money for each contract and the years in which to play. Now he had to convince Tank and the Boyagians to sign one! But the family had another option—and that was to sign both contracts and play for both teams when they didn't overlap. And overlaps wouldn't happen until springtime. So, if one team was out of contention for a playoff game, Tank would leave that team and continue with the one who was in contention.

Basketball season began on or about the third week in October, which meant that baseball season should have been finished by that time. Basketball ended in mid-April (unless that team was headed for the playoffs) when baseball would have just begun. If the Lakers were out of contention for a playoff spot, then Tank need not play another game for them and could concentrate and continue his play for the Angels.

A problem would only arise if the Lakers made the playoffs. Then the two teams' games would overlap, creating an issue with one or both teams. If the Angels weren't that concerned about Tank playing for them in April and May, they could just suspend Tank's salary for those months until he returned. But if the Angels wanted to cause a problem for Tank, they could release him outright and destroy his career in baseball. The Lakers could do the same. This created a kind of conundrum for Tank but only if the Lakers went into the playoffs. They had done so recently but were gone in the first round.

There was a good chance that Tank would sign both contracts but only at the behest of his parents and both leagues. Not surprisingly, with the blessing of his parents and the leagues, Tank signed both contracts, aiming to start first with the Lakers.

Both teams had come to an understanding of how they would proceed if the Lakers made the playoffs.

Tank would play baseball only when the Lakers had days off, and vice versa.

The managers made Tank sign both contracts in front of the news media—both local and international—and in the presence of both general managers from both teams and Tank's parents.

Tank couldn't understand what all the fuss was about. He had seen it before. It wasn't new to him.

***

Tank would start earning his pay by first playing with the LA Lakers. Before his first game began, the team made it a day Tank would remember forever by inviting and introducing, on the court, his brothers, parents, and even Hazel, his nanny and interpreter. Small bobble-heads of him were given to every fan that came to the game.

When Tank came out to practice in his new gold-and-blue practice uniform, the crowd went wild.

As the Lakers starting lineup was introduced, the crowd roared loudest when the announcer called out Tank's name and position.

"And last, but not least," the announcer shouted, "starting at Center for the LA Lakers, Tank Boyagian."

Tank stood up from his chair and rambled onto the floor, high-fiving his teammates. LeBron, hanging his head and listening to the burst of clapping and yelling for their new Center, seemed jealous of Tank.

Minutes later, the game started. Tank won the tipoff and tipped it to LeBron, who dribbled it up the court. Tank set himself up under the basket and nudged the opposing center just long enough to get in the clear and catch a pass from LeBron. Without leaving the floor, Tank slam dunked the ball hard—setting the stage for what was to come.

The crowd saw the dunk and went wild. As soon as the ball went into the basket, and before the ball hit the floor, Tank was already at the other end of the court, getting there even before LeBron.

After the game, the fans raved about Tank and the Lakers' lopsided win. They had beat the opposing team by 35 points. Tank was the hero of the game as he'd had the most three-pointers, blocked shots, rebounds, assists, and total points. He'd also hit 98 percent of his shots from the foul line. Tank beat LeBron in all categories, making LeBron look bad—or so LeBron thought.

The Lakers were 16 and 0 in their first 16 games with Tank at center, and that was the beginning of the end of Tank playing basketball. His stint stopped after 16 games because LeBron wanted him gone. Tank was making more plays, blocking more shots, and scoring more points than LeBron and the rest of his teammates together. The others didn't seem to mind that Tank was getting all the recognition for their winning streak, but LeBron thought Tank was making him look bad.

LeBron called Tank a "ball hog." To say the least, LeBron was jealous of Tank and wanted nothing to do with him off the court. At first, the two were "buddy-buddy," but that changed as Tank progressed to playing a better game than LeBron and winning every game he played in.

The kicker came when Tank scored 72 points against the Warriors and the Lakers won by double digits. Tank then scored 65 points against the Pistons and 56 points, 12 assists, and 13 blocked shots against the Boston Celtics. Again, he shot 98 percent from the foul line.

Tank was teaching the game to LeBron. LeBron couldn't stand it, but the fans loved the game Tank played.

The Lakers, due to Tank being on the team, were able to raise prices by 40 percent, with no complaints from the fans. Even the sports writers were pushing for the Lakers to sign Tank to a multi-year long-term contract to keep him a Laker for the next eight to ten years.

After Tank's sixteenth game, which was a home game, he decided to give something back to the fans, so he stayed late giving out his hand-print autograph. He refused to shower until the last fan had his autograph.

Tank was the last player to shower and dress. By the time Tank dressed in his handmade Superfly threads, it was nearly 2 a.m. Tank met Hazel at the door and headed to her car—the last car in the player's parking lot.

As Hazel unlocked her car door, the four Indonesian gangsters suddenly appeared out of nowhere. They shot Tank up with tranquilizers from a tranquilizer gun, as their friends had done before, hoping to subdue and kidnap Tank.

Hazel tried to intervene by pulling the gangsters off Tank, but the thugs threw her down hard onto the concrete. Seeing that, Tank became enraged and suddenly reverted back to the wild animal he was. For some reason, Tank seemed to have built up a tolerance to the tranquilizer drugs. He began pummeling thug after thug, throwing them around as though they were rag dolls.

He threw the gangsters down onto the concrete and began jumping up and down on their bodies, to the point that they no longer moved. His jumping on their chests smashed their bodies and ribs into the ground. He pummeled their bodies one at a time, smashing his fists into their bloody faces. He then picked up their limp bodies by their heads and tried ripping their eyes from their eye sockets. He threw them on the ground again, all the while making a screeching, wailing sound as he jumped up and down on each of their bodies again and again.

In retrospect, the four Indonesian gangsters that had tried to kidnap Tank before these unfortunate ones and were deported had gotten off lucky.

Hazel was finally able to get up from the concrete and stood up to calm Tank down. She had never seen him like this before. He was scary in the frame of mind he was now in.

Both Hazel and Tank were distracted, so neither saw one of the now dying gangsters pull a small thirty-two caliber pistol from an ankle holster. The gangster shot Tank in the chest, knocking him down to the ground and adding Tank's body to theirs.

Hazel called for an ambulance, hoping it would get there in time to save Tank's life. She knew that Tank had just saved her life by taking a bullet in the chest.

The police and the ambulance arrived, and Tank was on his way to the hospital. The four gangsters were on their way to the morgue. Tank had won that game too!

Hazel phoned the Boyagians to tell them about Tank and his injuries. She followed the ambulance to the hospital and watched as the medical staff wheeled him into the emergency room and then into the operating room.

The surgeons would do everything possible to save Tank's life. Tank represented the divine connection between God and humanity which is called the tree of life. It signifies hope, renewal and the promise of God's love. Tank was the tree of life for nearly every kid in LA and of most kids in California, so they had to save his life at all cost. Even though they weren't veterinarians, they vowed to do their very best to save him.

***

The Boyagians arrived at the hospital, and they were immediately allowed to assist in Tank's operation. A CT scan of Tank's chest revealed that the bullet had splintered into four small pieces. One piece had landed just millimeters from his heart and its main artery, and another piece had pierced his lung, which had collapsed. The other two pieces were easy to get at and not detrimental to Tank's health. Nevertheless, it would take steady hands to retrieve the pieces of lead without doing major damage.

Mariam Boyagian was given the chance to operate on her son, and she accepted. She had saved his life when he was two months old, and now she would do it again. She wasn't about to fail. Her husband would assist her, and the other doctors stayed for support.

Mariam was able to retrieve three of the lead pieces without any issues. However, she saw that the remaining piece of shrapnel—the one that had pierced his lung—was going to be a problem.

She had to retrieve the BB-sized shrapnel and then suture the hole if Tank was going to mend properly. After a nearly six-hour-long operation, all signs were positive.

During the operation, Tank lost a lot of blood, so they had to pump seven ounces into him to jump-start his bodily functions. All his organs were in fine shape, and luckily, over the years, the Boyajians had taken a few ounces of blood from Tank each year to be used in emergency situations like this one.

The availability of Tank's own blood and his parents' expertise in the field of medicine most likely saved his life. After the operation, he was still in critical condition and was moved to the ICU. Now, he had to rest.

The first night after surgery was critical. If Tank made it through the night, that would be a good sign that he would come out of the shooting okay.

***

The Lakers' Press Corp put out a conciliatory message wishing Tank the best during his recuperation and hoping he would get well soon. They thanked him for the time spent on the court and for giving everything he had. Their message ended with the following: *Will keep the fans updated on Tank's condition weekly. Thank you.*

After three weeks in the hospital, Tank was doing fine and was moved to his family home.

***

With Tank away from the court, the Lakers were on a losing streak! With Tank playing, the Lakers had won 16 straight games and lost none. Without him, their record was four in the winning column and 24 in the losing column. Without Tank in the game, the players had no passion, no will to play! Everyone on the team needed and wanted Tank—everyone, that is, except LeBron James. LeBron could not care less whether Tank returned to the Lakers or not.

***

Tank was hoping to play basketball again as soon as he was able. His shoulders and arms were stiff and not yet limber enough to play any sports, let alone basketball. He was still bedridden after a month but would soon start rehab to strengthen his arms. He needed to work on his arms so he could dunk the ball without any problems or swing the bat with enough power to hit the ball where they ain't—and that was into the stands for home runs. And he needed to strengthen his leg muscles so he could run up and down the court or run around bases.

Tank promised to get back into the same shape he'd been in before the shooting. And after three months of excruciating rehabilitation, Tank was ready to return to the court. It was time!

***

Tank soon discovered that during the time he'd been away from the game, his Lakers contract had been bought back by the Lakers for 120 million dollars and paid to the Boyagians and Tank's agent. Tank had been released from his contract, and according to the Lakers' front office, this was due to his injuries from the beating he had taken and the bullet he had stopped.

That wasn't the real reason, however. A story was leaked that LeBron had refused to play if Tank was allowed to return.

"Let him go play baseball!" was all LeBron would say.

Chapter 15

ank didn't understand what had happened and why they wouldn't allow him to play basketball.

"Why? Do I do bad?" Tank signed to Hazel.

Once again, Tank was saddened. This was the third time a sports team had gotten rid of him. Since he now had time on his hands until baseball season, he decided to do what he had done before, and that was to teach his students again. The football thing had been a bad idea and a complete bust. His students just hadn't had the knack for it.

In the meantime, other basketball teams were wanting Tank on their teams, provided he could pass their physicals. In addition to the other NBA teams wanting Tank as an addition to their teams, Tank's agent also had professional soccer teams wondering if Tank might be available to play soccer. A video of Tank playing soccer with his brothers while visiting them at college had emerged, showing Tank to be a terror on the field and as a goalkeeper. He could kick a ball from one goal to the other.

However, soccer would interfere with baseball season, as its season began in February and playoff games began in October, ending in December! So soccer would also interfere with basketball, should he decide to sign with a different basketball team. If he signed with another basketball team, his agent would need to arrange an agreement similar to one Tank had had with the Lakers and Angels concerning overlapping games.

Tank's agent decided to listen to the basketball owners from eight different teams to possibly negotiate a contract for Tank. The eight teams wanting to hire Tank were the Chicago Bulls, Detroit Pistons, LA Clippers, Sacramento Kings, Phoenix Suns, Utah Jazz, New Orleans Pelicans, and Portland Trailblazers.

After speaking with Tank and the Boyagians, the agent realized that Tank and his family wanted him to stay close to home. So, the agent recommended that they pick the one team that met that qualification. That team was the LA Clippers, the nemesis of the LA Lakers.

The agent set up a time and date for him and Tank to meet with the owner, general manager, and teammates. Tank didn't need to show them his game. They knew how great he was, as he had beaten and dominated them in the two games he'd played against them. Tank had scored over 40 points in each of those games.

In the 16 games he'd played for the LA Lakers, Tank had averaged 42 points a game, 18 rebounds, 10 assists, and 12 blocked shots per game. And he'd shot 96 percent of the time from the free throw line. He set the bar quite high!

The LA Clippers were a decent and winning team, but the addition of Tank would move them up a notch from second best in their division to first. They were likely to be able to overtake the Lakers with Tank's help. He likely would add 15 to 20 wins for the Clippers.

Tank and his agent met with the powers that be for the Clippers. The negotiation went well, as they offered 900 million dollars for 12 years and an additional 500 million dollar five-year extension, for which he would receive 100 million dollars for each year played after his 12-year contract expired. That would add up to a total of one billion, four-hundred thousand dollars over a 17 year period. He also had the Clippers agree that if baseball interfered with basketball playoffs, Tank would play in their playoff games and only play baseball when the Clippers didn't play.

Tank would now be the highest paid player in the NBA, if he decided to sign the contract. Between the two teams Tank would earn a total of 1.52 billion dollars over a 17 year career, assuming that he played all 17 years and did not get hurt during that time.

After the agent had spoken with the Boyagians and Tank, all were happy with the deal. That day, the agent was able to get the Boyagians' signatures and Tank's handprint on the contract.

Tank was happy to dominate the game of basketball once again. He promised his new teammates that he'd take them to a National Championship, but not until October, when basketball season started. He didn't want to start in the middle of the season, and it looked like the Clippers were going into the playoffs. If he joined the team in mid-season, he wouldn't be able to start for his baseball team. And right now, he wanted to concentrate on a complete season playing baseball for the Angels. Then, in October, he'd join the Clippers.

Tank was committed to baseball, as the season was about to begin, and he wanted desperately to get the team into the playoffs. His manager, Ray Montgomery, believed Tank could hit 75 to 90 home runs in a season with at least 150 RBIs. They had great expectations with Tank. They expected a 300+ batting average from him, an All Star stint, and at least 40 home runs by All Star break. So Tank decided to concentrate all his efforts toward baseball.

When basketball season started in October, Tank would join the Clippers. However, Tank would soon be heading to the Angels spring training camp at Tempe Diablo Stadium in Tempe, Arizona. The time there would hone his skill level even better and would help get him in even better shape than he already was.

Hazel, of course, would travel with him on the road and at home. The Clippers' arena was only a few miles from the new mansion the Boyagians had built from the settlement they'd received from the Lakers buyback of Tank's contract. Along with their new mansion, they'd also had their Boyagian Veterinary Clinic expanded to twice the size. The total cost had been less than 0.1 percent of the buyout.

The Boyagians hadn't forgotten about Tank or his brothers. Their mansion included a professional batting cage and a full basketball court that was as well-made as any used in the NBA.

Tank's brothers, now part of his company, ran the marketing, product line, and investments. Jerome was the CEO of the company while the others were heads of the different departments within the company. They were all doing what was in the best interest of Tank and his company. They loved doing this for their hairy brother.

***

At the end of February, the Angels representative picked Tank and Hazel up in the CEO's limousine and had them taken to John Wayne airport for a flight to

Tempe, Arizona in the team's executive private Lear jet. They arrived at their destination 75 minutes later.

There, a representative had them taken by limousine to their hotel, where the hotel manager showed them to their rooms. Each was a beautiful four-room suite with a kitchenette. The Angels management had stuffed Tank's room with a week's worth of the special food he liked, including shrubs, roots, bushes, flowers, and lots and lots of fruits of all kinds. Tank loved the special attention he was getting and thanked the representative for it.

Tank and Hazel rested up for the rest of the evening due to jet lag. They would be taken to Diablo Stadium the next day by the same Angels representative that had traveled with them from Los Angeles, but not before they had eaten breakfast.

After breakfast, the Angels representative came to bring them to the ballpark. Before leaving, Tank grabbed his mitt and the bat he'd had specially made by Louisville Slugger but which first had to be inspected by the league. Tank's bat was bigger, longer, and heavier than any bat ever made for a major league ballplayer. But then Tank wasn't your average ballplayer. He was bigger, heavier, taller, and hairier than any other major league ballplayer.

As the limousine passed the gates to the parking lot for the players, the representative showed both Hazel and

Tank the clubhouse and Tank's cubicle that contained a half-dozen new uniforms but left little room for his other effects. He still had enough room for his baseball shoes, special bat, and a place to hang his hat, but barely. But no matter, this made Tank very happy, as was Hazel.

Within minutes, Tank's teammates began rolling into the clubhouse. Each gave Tank a heartfelt pat on the back or arm. Everyone was tickled pink to see the hairy one, and he, in turn, was happy to see them.

When visiting the dugout, Tank was shown a dozen of his special bats in the bat rack, along with three batting helmets and two specially made gloves for his extra-large hands. He gave a loud grunt to show his happiness with these baseball effects. Those there laughed at Tank's response to his baseball equipment.

Hazel was given a seat in the dugout, just in case she needed to interpret any questions that Tank might have for the coach and others. Furthermore, Tank needed to learn the signs for running the bases in case the ball he hit didn't go over the fences but instead fell in play for a double or triple. That was an important part of the game, and Tank needed to learn it. Over time, he'd learn.

For batting practice, however, he had nothing to learn. His swing was dead on. Each pitch was hit over the fences at distances of 450 feet or better, with two going over 500 feet. He was hitting just as he had done before being signed. TB hadn't lost his touch.

The next step was that he needed to pass his physical. The Angel front office knew he would pass because he had passed his physicals for both his football and basketball days. So they had no qualms that passing the physical would be a problem for Tank, even though he hadn't had one since being beaten and shot on that fateful day. And they knew what they were talking about because Tank passed the league's physical with flying colors.

During practice, Tank would sometimes pitch batting practice. While fooling around, his catcher wanted him to throw a fastball over the plate as fast as he could throw it. Tank did so, and the ball was clocked over the plate at 102 mph. The manager had him do that again, and Tank did it with a fastball clocked at 100.2 mph. He knew how to throw a fastball, as well as two-seam and four-seam fastballs, an 89 mph slider, a 75 mph slow curve, and an 84 mph changeup, and he even knew how to throw a knuckle ball. All these pitches he had learned from his brothers while in elementary, middle, and high school, when they would play ball together after school.

Even when the brothers were in college, they continued to play baseball games with the hairy one, and they all enjoyed it immensely. They taught Tank well.

Tank was as good as, if not better than, the Angels' starting pitchers. The Angels manager decided to add Tank to the starting roster of starting pitchers. They would use Tank as their fifth starting pitcher in the rotation.

The front office signed Tank as a power hitter for an outrageous amount of money. Now, however, Tank could add starting pitcher to his resume. His agent would surely ask for additional funds once Tank pitched in his first game. That was just good business.

***

After daily practices for a month, Tank had become an even better player. He soaked in everything he had seen, including how the other starting pitchers threw their pitches. They gave him the secrets to their pitches, which he added to his repertoire, and they also promised to tell him about the opposing batters and vulnerable pitches to strike them out with. Tank took all this knowledge and used it to his benefit, but he changed nothing as far as his actions in the batter's box.

Only time would tell if Tank would make a difference and earn his pay. And time did tell, from his first game played to his last.

Opening day for Tank and the Angels went on essentially as planned. The Angels won the game, with Tank's help, of course. He went 4 for 4, hitting two home runs, one grand slam, and two doubles, hitting a total of six RBIs.

By the time the All Star game rolled around, Tank was nearing the 40 home run mark and had the highest votes to earn himself an All Star spot as designated hitter (DH). He was also the only player on his team to earn a spot by helping his team win 53 games against only 30 losses.

Tank was sad that none of his other teammates had been selected to play in the All Star game but he was happy to be part of it and show off his best qualities there, including hitting for power, especially home runs. They called Tank the new "Shohei Ohtani."

Chapter 16

Two games before the last game of the season, Tank was beaned by a 102 mph fastball to the head. It knocked off his helmet and knocked him out cold before he hit the ground hard.

The team's trainer ran onto the field to check out their best player. The umpire believed the pitch was a deliberate and intentional attempt to get Tank out of the game. At that point in the game, Tank had hit a 500 foot home run, a 420 foot home run, and two doubles, giving him six RBIs.

The umpire threw the pitcher out of the game. Most likely, the player would be suspended by the league for the rest of the season and fined six figures or more, depending on how badly and seriously Tank had been hurt.

Tank was taken to the hospital by ambulance for observation and an MRI. He regained consciousness just as they were loading him into the ambulance. That was always a good sign.

Tank was in the hospital for the last two days of the regular season, diagnosed with a concussion from the impact of the 102 mph baseball hitting the side of his head. The team missed the playoffs by one game, even though Tank had taken them from a 60-game winning season the last year to an 85-game winning season this year. He'd also hit 64 home runs, 160 RBIs, and had a .325 era. He'd also had 12 wins and two losses as a starting pitcher and was also in the running for MVP.

***

While the Angels finished up their season, Tank was released from the hospital after four days of observation. He would now have to report to the Clippers management for a league physical and practice. Fortunately, Tank passed this physical as he had all others—with flying colors.

Once on the practice court, Tank showed his dominance. He hadn't lost a step, even though he'd been out of basketball for over a year. Tank wasn't called a "sports phenom" for nothing. Whichever sport he played, he was always nothing short of great.

The first game of the season was against the Clippers' nemesis, LeBron and the LA Lakers. The Clippers won by 26 points, 130–104.

Tank scored 56 points on that night alone. After 40 games, he averaged 48 points per game, with 22 rebounds, 14 blocked shots, and 6 assists. And he shot 100 percent from the foul line.

The Clippers' record to this point was 42 wins against three losses. The three games lost were by one point, and the opponents had taken the last shot with less than one second left on the clock.

Tank was torn between two loves: wanting to play baseball for a complete season and wanting to continue with the Clippers for the remaining games (around 40 games before the playoffs). If he went to spring training, he would miss the rest of the Clippers' season.

Tank had promised to play in the All Star game in mid-February, but he wanted out after that game to go to spring training in Arizona with the Angels. He wanted his agent to work something out. However, his agent reminded him that they had hashed out an agreement in the contract that he had signed that he would play baseball when the Clippers weren't playing and play basketball when they were.

Tank was anxious to get to spring training with Trout and all his teammates. He told his agent something that surprised even the agent. Tank wanted back into the NFL so he could play both football and baseball without the teams' games overlapping.

Tank was reminded once again that he had played only a few months of basketball for the Clippers and was still under the 12-year contract that he had signed and had made him the highest-paid NBA player—EVER!

Money really didn't matter to Tank. That was for his parents and his brothers. He just wanted to be happy playing the sports he loved. And right now, he didn't love basketball because it was stopping him from playing baseball.

But what could Tank do? He had a 12-year contract with the Clippers, who were headed to the playoffs. That would interfere with his baseball career.

So his agent spoke with both front offices and worked out an agreement with the Angels and Clippers.

The Angels felt that Tank didn't need to get in shape and could miss spring training.

The Clippers, if they did make the playoffs, would surely get a bye in the first round, so they wouldn't start the playoffs until the last week in May. The All Star game was a weeklong event, so after playing the game, Tank could return to play a few games with the Angels before returning to play for the Clippers.

Tank was unhappy with this outcome. He again told his agent that he would rather play football and baseball, not baseball and basketball. It wouldn't be so bad if the Clippers didn't make the playoffs, but Tank wouldn't allow that to happen. He only played to win and always gave 110 percent effort.

***

What people didn't understand was that Tank's agent was having meetings with Commissioner Goodell. Goodell had propositioned him with an offer for Tank to once again play in the NFL.

Tank's agent was floored, to say the least. Goodell had suspended Tank for being too good and had vowed never to allow Tank to play in the NFL again. He had then told Tank to try the USFL. So when Goodell telephoned Tank's agent with the proposition, the agent was flabbergasted and nearly fell out of his chair.

Tank's agent then set up a meeting with himself, Goodell, and Steve Ballmer, the owner of the Clippers. They all met in Commissioner Goodell's office.

Tank's agent told Mr. Ballmer that Tank was unhappy playing professional basketball only because it interfered with his playing professional baseball. Tank still loved playing the game for the Clippers, but he wanted to pursue a baseball career instead and he hoped that one day he would also be able to get back into the NFL. Football was Tank's first love. His second love was baseball.

Ballmer brought up Tank's contractual agreement to play for the Clippers for the next 12 years. And he mentioned how they made Tank the highest paid NBA player in the history of the game.

Goodell asked Ballmer what it would take to release Tank from his contract.

Ballmer thought for a minute and said, "You'll have to buy out Tank's Clippers' contract and provide for the losses were sure to have without Tank in the game. If he quits now, we may not even make it to the playoffs. So, the Clippers will want at least 1.5 billion dollars, the same amount for his contract and five year extension. He could take us all the way to win a National Championship. But if we lose him now, the Clippers will falter. Tank's one of a kind!"

"Don't I know it," said Goodell, with a sheepish smirk.

Tank's agent figured there was no deal to be had. But this was only the first meeting of many in the days and weeks to come. At least the cards were on the table for all to see.

Goodell told the agent and Ballmer that he would speak to the owners to see whether they felt that Tank was worth that amount of money to the NFL. The cost to the NFL to revoke Tank's Clippers contract was 1.5 billion dollars, but Tank's play in the NFL was worth a good 5 billion dollars PER SEASON, as Tank put fans into the stadiums and increased NFL revenue from sponsors when negotiating with the networks for both

TV, radio, and Internet advertising. Tank's name alone was worth 5 billion.

***

Tank was already back in the headlines of local, national, and international media. And the coverage went on for weeks, with all waiting to see if a deal could be made.

The basketball fanatics were adamant that Ballmer should not sell Tank at all, especially for the pittance being asked for his extraordinary play. Tank was worth four times the amount that the NFL was paying for him.

The football fanatics were adamant that Tank was worth the money at any cost and that even paying 2 billion dollars was a bargain, especially when Tank had at least a 15 to 20-year football career ahead of him.

Tank, at the very least, would make a cool 5 to 6 billion dollars a year for the NFL and its affiliates. Multiply that by 15 or 20 years and that made a great deal for Goodell, Tank's agent, the Boyagians, and Tank himself, and the NFL's TV ratings would go through the roof. That ratings increase alone was worth a good 5 billion dollars every year on its own, especially when dealing with the stations.

Goodell told Ballmer and Tank's agent that he'd get back with them after meeting with the NFL owners. Two weeks to the day, they met once again.

The agent hoped Goodell would have some good news for him and Tank. Ballmer wouldn't be happy under any circumstances, and neither would the fans. Ballmer, as the former co-founder and CEO of Microsoft, really didn't care about the money. He'd paid 2.5 billion dollars for the Clippers more than 10 years ago, which was 1.5 times more than it was worth, but Ballmer had been willing to pay whatever it took to get a basketball franchise. And he was lucky enough to be in the right place at the right time to get an LA franchise.

In Anaheim, the home of Angels fans, the Angels' owner, Arte Moreno, was happy to have the NFL acquire Tank's contract from the Clippers, who didn't want to lose Tank, but would if the deal was good for all sides.

The Clippers, before Tank, had still been a winning ball club, second only to the Lakers. So Ballmer would take the money and invest it in other great players, but only if Goodell was hungry enough to invest in the NFL's future. Ballmer believed that Tank would never again play professional basketball if he could play his two most favorite sports: football and baseball.

Ballmer was right. Goodell signed a check for nearly two billion dollars to the Clippers organization.

Now Tank could play both baseball and football, just like Bo Jackson had back in the late eighties and early nineties before a hip fracture knocked the wind out of his sails. And Tank could quit worrying about overlapping games. He could concentrate now strictly on baseball.

When the agent told Tank the outcome of the meeting, Mariam signed the agent's words to Tank to ensure that he understood. Tank went berserk, but in a happy way, pacing around the room slowly at first and then faster, flailing his arms above his head and screeching, grunting, and yelling at first in a normal voice and then in a squeaky voice. He went over to both parents and hugged them lovingly and then did the same to Hazel.

After a few minutes of Tank's "dancing in the streets," he finally calmed down and sat down in his favorite chair. He was so happy about being allowed back into the NFL.

All Tank could sign was "me, good boy" and he patted himself on his chest.

The networks and other media outlets went hog wild over the NFL's decision to allow Tank to play football once again. The LA Times headlines for nearly a week ran with: Sports Phenom allowed in the NFL Again.

The article below the headline mentioned that no team had been selected to buy Tank's contract outright. Many in the betting world decided to form a consortium of a half dozen investors—all billionaires who would pitch in and pay whatever monies Commissioner Goodell and the NFL decided upon.

However, Goodell threw a wrench into the gearbox. He decided he would auction off Tank to the highest bidder. The team that bid the highest dollar amount for Tank's abilities and expertise would win.

The LA Rams, with their rich investor backing, were ready for the auction that night and would bid until it hurt! They figured that the purchase of Tank's contract could go as high as 3 to 5 billion dollars and possibly even higher. The team that won Tank's employment would assuredly get to the Super Bowl.

Tank couldn't be stopped on offensive play or defensive play. He was the "real deal," and everyone had seen that during his play with the Titans. The Titans would also be in the running for Tank's football prowess, but 3 to 5 billion dollars for Tank's services was a bit much for the Titans. They didn't have the billionaire backers and funds the other teams had, like the New York Jets, Rams, Chargers or even San Francisco 49ers. The Titans promised their fans that they would do their best against the big boys.

***

One team had sinister reasons behind their desire to acquire Tank. When the four still-living Indonesian gangsters heard about the auction, they invested over 800 million dollars into a team that was cash depleted, thereby gaining a 71 percent majority stake in that team. They now hoped to win the auction and reap the rewards, as they would use Tank to make TV and radio commercials for more than 200 different products. This could add over 500 million to one billion dollars to their coffers each and every year for the next 12 years at least.

But these potential new owners weren't really interested in Tank's abilities and expertise. They hadn't forgotten that Tank had killed four members of their gang. They wanted revenge for their friends' deaths.

They wanted to do what their friends had failed to do, but they no longer wanted to auction him off to their billionaire friends who were into Monkey Brain Consumption. Now, they just wanted Tank dead—and at any cost! They would assassinate him, even if it was done during the day, out in the open, or in front of others. Any one of them would sacrifice their life to take Tank's, even if it meant living for the rest of their lives sitting in an eight foot by six foot prison cell.

However, before the gangsters could act, their plans were foiled when ICE intercepted them. They had all overstayed their visas by more than four months. All were arrested on misdemeanors, but when frisked, they were found carrying illegal firearms with filed down serial numbers.

The four gangsters were thrown in jail and denied bond. They refused to plea bargain and took their cases to trial. All lost. Instead of three to five year sentences, they were given mandatory minimums of five to ten years and then another year each, to run consecutively, for overstaying their visas. Once released, they would be met by ICE agents at the prison gate and put on a flight back to Indonesia.

Chapter 17

The auction went off without a hitch and was even televised on local, national, and international stations because there was so much interest from football fans from the US and around the world. Everyone wanted to see if their favorite team would be lucky enough to win Tank's services—his heart and soul—for the next 12 years. They all hoped that Tank would take their teams to the promised land and get them a Super Bowl Championship! They knew that whoever won Tank's employment would, no doubt, go all the way!

All the NFL teams were bidding on live television. The auction was over in less than one hour. The dollar amount went to 9 billion dollars before bidding slowed. Just three teams remained in the running: the Rams, the Chargers, and San Francisco. All California teams.

When the auction had begun, bidding had started in ten million dollar increments, but then the New York Jets started bidding in 100 million dollar increments. That took the auction to another level for smaller teams.

When the bidding reached 7 billion dollars, all but five teams had dropped out. Two minutes later, the bidding was at 8 billion dollars. That was too much for the New York Jets and the San Francisco 49ers. The only teams remaining were the Rams and Chargers and the Seattle Seahawks.

Seattle soon dropped out when the bid hit 9 billion dollars. That left the Rams and Chargers in the race to secure Tank's employment.

From there, one bid later, the Rams offered 10 billion dollars. That was just too much for the Chargers and Coach Harbaugh.

Harbaugh wanted Tank on his team more than anything. As a rookie coach, he had coached his team to a winning season and into the playoffs but then they lost in the first round. He was sure that Tank could get them to the promised land. But it wasn't to be.

After a long and strenuous bidding war, the Rams became the victors.

***

The Chargers front office, to say the least, were dejected. The Rams front office, however, was elated at winning Tank's services for at least the next 12 years. And the Boyagian family was definitely elated, as they were fanatical Rams fans. The Rams would have no trouble getting their approval from them, Tank's agent, or Tank.

The Boyagian family were in celebration mode, knowing that Tank would only have to travel a few miles to the stadium for home games, with Hazel traveling with him for both home and away games, as she had before.

The Rams had paid five times the amount of money than Goodell had, which meant buying Tank's contract not only made a big profit for the NFL, but would soon make a bigger profit for the Rams.

The Rams also knew that Tank's abilities far outnumbered their Hall of Fame players' abilities. No one could hold a candle to Tank. That's what had gotten Tank suspended from the NFL in the first place. Tank was too good. Goodell didn't care anymore if Tank made other great players look bad.

This time around, it was Tank's turn. Those others would just have to step up their game if they wanted to compete against Tank. That was a given!

Tank's abilities and expertise in football hadn't changed. Tank was a franchise all by himself. In games past, he had made 70 percent of the plays, scored 90 percent of the touchdowns, had 99 percent of the quarterback sacks, and created and recovered 90 percent of the fumbles.

The NFL's front office didn't care about other players or teams whining that Tank was too good. That didn't cut it anymore. The owners knew the rules and had voted with Goodell to bring Tank back into the NFL. And the Rams now had the good fortune to have Tank on their team for the next 12 years and it had only cost them a measly 10 billion dollars. Plus, they could extend his contract for an additional five years for just another 100 million dollars a year, which meant they would have a winning team for 17 years, as long as Tank stayed healthy. He'd surely take the Rams to the Super Bowl and win it all.

The majority of Las Vegas bettors had the Rams winning next year's Super Bowl and the next six consecutive Super Bowls. They had two bets at one dollar to win one million dollars that the Rams would win 17 consecutive Super Bowls.

The news media all over the world made this story even bigger than Tank himself. The LA Times headlines read: Sports Phenom 10 Billion Dollar Boy!

The article below the headlines talked about how the Rams were surely headed to the Super Bowl for many years to come. The news media had as much confidence in Tank's abilities as Goodell and the NFL had.

The news media had been reporting on Tank from his midget days to his professional football and hockey days. Now, they looked forward to Tank's baseball days. They hadn't seen him play much baseball, but they were certain that he was as good at baseball as he was at football and hockey. Tank was special. One of a kind.

Critics said that the media hyped Tank's abilities in football, but reporters were quick to point out Tank's statistics, not only for football, but for hockey and basketball. That's why the media called him a "Sports Phenom."

***

Tank was happy that he would be playing football for his favorite team, the Los Angeles Rams. But now he had to get ready to play baseball for the Los Angeles Angels.

A month later, Tank and Hazel were in Tempe, Arizona, for spring training. Everyone, including the media, were anxiously waiting to see if Tank was as good at baseball as he was at football. The Angels' players knew how good Tank was at hitting. They remembered Tank hitting home run after home run during last year's season.

The Angels had won 30 games more with Tank than they had without him. They hoped they could win even more games. Las Vegas betting houses had the Angels winning their division and making the playoffs. The House was giving the Angels five to two odds of making it to the World Series.

The Angels Opening Day went as planned. Tank was the starting pitcher and designated hitter. He pitched a no-hitter going into the eighth inning and went three for three at the plate, with three home runs; all were hit well over 450 feet.

The manager relieved Tank for the ninth inning, with the Angels leading 6–0 and finally winning the game 6–1.

The Angels season went just like the last year's season, except this year they won their division and led the league with 108 wins. Tank hit for a .350 average, hit 68 home runs, and won 18 games and lost two as a pitcher.

Tank took his team to the World Series, only to be beaten by the Los Angeles Dodgers in seven games. Tank won the three games that he pitched and beat Ohtani in home runs at 14–7 and RBIs at 22–3. That last statistic, however, wasn't really fair to Ohtani because he was the Dodgers' leadoff hitter.

***

With the baseball season over, Tank was ready to suit up for his new football team, the Los Angeles Rams. He had played against them once during his time in the NFL before being suspended. Now that Tank was allowed to play in the NFL again, he was going to make the best of it.

The Rams' first game was against Harbaugh and the Chargers. Tank and Hazel arrived at the Rams clubhouse a few hours earlier than usual, but it was Opening Day.

The team had kept Tank out of the preseason games so they could decide which players needed to be cut to reach their limit of 53. However, out of those 53, only 46 were allowed to dress for games. The other seven were on the roster but couldn't play.

Tank would start as halfback on offense and play defensive linebacker and sometimes right tackle. For Opening Day kickoff, Tank was sent out with "Special Teams."

The kickoff went straight to Tank. He caught the ball on the Rams' eight yard line. He ran the ball into the Chargers' end zone but the play was called back due to a holding penalty. That happened a lot to Tank. He would run the ball from one end of the field to the other, from end zone to end zone, and more times than not, the play would be called back for, usually, a holding penalty by one of his offensive linemen. Had those penalties not occurred, Tank's statistics in touchdowns and yards made would have doubled or tripled in a season.

For the next play, Tank ordered his teammates not to block at all. He would clear the way for a touchdown. They did as ordered and when the ball was snapped, the quarterback handed it off to Tank. Tank tucked the ball tightly into his midsection and ran with 500 pounds of fury. He just pushed aside three of the defensive line and had an open field. He ran from the Rams' four yard line all the way to the Chargers' six yard line but was tripped up at the last moment by a lucky linebacker who grabbed Tank's ankle to bring him down. This didn't happen very often.

Tank usually carried three or four opposing players on his back and around his legs, as they tried to stop him from scoring a touchdown. This time, he was stopped by having his ankle grabbed. The next play called was the same: give the ball to Tank and let him run it into the end zone. This time, he did.

Four plays later, the Chargers had to kick the ball from their 20 yard line. The kicker kicked a high, looping ball that Tank caught. He plowed through the opposing players like a semi-truck plowing through parked cars. But just before he ran into the Chargers' end zone, that same linebacker was able to grab hold of Tank's right ankle and again tripped him up. That stopped Tank on the Chargers' four yard line.

Tank hit the ground hard. He was slow getting up. When he did stand, the fans could tell that Tank had sprained his right ankle and had to be helped off the field.

Tank sat on the sidelines for the rest of the game, with bags of ice wrapped around his swollen ankle. The Rams didn't want to take any chances with their 10 billion dollar man. But without Tank in the game, the

Rams lost by a field goal in the last seconds of the game. The final score was 24–21 for the Chargers.

Tank took the loss hard. He always played to win. At least now he had a week to rest his ankle before playing the Detroit Lions at home.

Chapter 18

During that week of resting, Nike had made a special Tank shoe, not only for him, but also for sale in retail shops for the fans. They made a basketball shoe, a baseball shoe, and a football shoe. They were similar to the "Jordan" shoe, but made strictly for Tank, with his logo on each pair. They were beautiful and had the backing of Tank, his brothers, and his parents.

Tank and his brothers made commercials for the shoes, which added to Tank's wealth. And the media couldn't get enough of him. He was in the headlines in the sports section nearly every day. His prowess on the field and his love for the game and his family were second to none. And he showed it by having his brothers on the sidelines with him at home games and his parents close by in the stands.

***

Tank's ankle was fine for the game against the Lions. The Rams' trainer gave Tank a "thumbs up" and allowed him to play. And Tank was ready. He was more than ready. Having sat out for most of the game the week before, he was pumped up for this game. His parents were close by in the stands, even though they were given their own enclosed box with all the same amenities as the owner's enclosed box, but was closer to their star. However, by sitting in the stands, George and Mariam could keep an eye on Tank's brothers and Hazel, just in case they were needed for an emergency.

***

Tank dressed and went out onto the field with all his other teammates to warm up and practice before the game started.

Tank really was earning his keep. This was the second game at SoFi stadium and it was filled to the rafters, with "Standing Room Only." SoFi had a seating capacity of over 70,000 seats but could accommodate over 100,000 fans with "SRO." And wanting to catch a glimpse of Tank, over 30,000 fans were willing to stand for the whole game. That made more money for the food vendors, the clothing vendors, and other vendors within the ballpark, and for other businesses in the city, such as restaurants and parking lots, which were overflowing with fans and cars. Each home game earned them a big chunk of their yearly pay by serving a big chunk of those 100,000 fans.

This game was against the Lions—one of the top three teams to be picked by Las Vegas odds makers to get to the Super Bowl.

The game against the Lions went as expected. It began with the fans getting their money's worth, but ended with the fans being shortchanged.

Right from the kickoff, the game went as planned, with the Rams going ahead by four touchdowns in the first eight minutes of the first quarter. Tank made all four touchdowns; three offensively, and one defensively. Two of the TDs he scored he ran from the Rams' twenty-five yard scrimmage line into the Lions' end zone within the first two minutes of the game. The third offensive TD Tank made was a play the fans hadn't seen before, which was a "Statue of Liberty" play.

The ball was snapped to the quarterback, and he acted like he was going to pass the ball to a receiver. He froze in that position until Tank grabbed the ball from his hand. Tank acted as though he was going to run with the ball, but he saw that he had an open receiver in the clear, 40 yards downfield, and he saw the defensive players running toward him. Tank suddenly passed the ball perfectly and hit his receiver, who ran the ball for a touchdown. Tank had thrown a perfect spiral pass sixty yards downfield to his receiver. The crowd cheered and went wild. The decibel level hit record highs, high enough that the noise could have blown out ear drums.

The fourth touchdown scored by Tank just minutes later was on the defensive side. Tank flew past the offensive line and hit the Lions quarterback hard enough that he knocked the ball out of the quarterback's hands, picked it up on the Lions' forty-five yard line, and ran it with two offensive linemen hanging onto each side of his back and one on each leg. They still couldn't stop him.

Nearing the Lions' ten yard line, the Lions' Center came running at full speed across the field, and clipped Tank's right leg and ankle. Tank fell hard onto the ground, and the ball landed between Tank's stomach and the ground. When Tank hit the ground, it knocked the wind out of him and knocked him unconscious. It looked maybe even worse because Tank didn't move.

The trainer came running out onto the field to check on Tank's injuries. When he came upon Tank, both the Lions and Rams players had surrounded Tank, wanting him to move and get up. But the trainer had them keep their distance and called for a stretcher and ambulance. When he couldn't get Tank to move, he had a few of the players help move Tank onto his back.

By the time Tank's parents, brothers, and Hazel had run onto the field, Tank had been unconscious for over six minutes. The ball had left a three inch depression in the ground. By the time the ambulance arrived, Tank had been unconscious for eleven minutes.

Four big burly guys, around 290 pounds each and a good six feet four inches tall or better, helped get Tank onto the stretcher and into the ambulance.

Just as they were hoisting him into the ambulance, Tank suddenly awakened and looked around confusedly.

Jerome bent down and whispered something into Tank's ear. Tank gave out a high-pitched grunt and then held up his thumb to give the "all clear" sign. The crowd noticed on the big screen that Tank was now conscious and okay, giving a "thumbs up" signal.

They placed Tank into the ambulance. His mother was allowed to ride with him to the hospital. She took his vitals with her stethoscope, but she noticed something strange. She thought that she was just overly excited and was overreacting, thinking the worst and hoping for the best. And with the noise from the tires on the road, she wasn't quite sure what she'd heard. She put the thought out of her mind and just sat and waited until they reached the hospital's emergency room.

She believed she had heard the same sounds a month or so before, when Tank had been beaned in the head by a vindictive opposing pitcher. But even then she had put the thought out of her head, believing she was just overworked and tired from the long days that she and her husband had been putting in since the remodeling and new addition had been built. She'd been working 18 to

20 hour days, seven days a week, without taking a vacation or break, so the faint noises she had heard before and now were just her head playing tricks on her.

To be on the safe side, she had Tank removed from the hospital to her veterinary hospital, as she'd done before. The radiology team had just put Tank into the MRI machine, but before they could get him to lie still to take an X-ray or MRI, they were ordered to wheel Tank out of the MRI room and to the waiting room. Tank would be transferred from the human hospital to the animal hospital.

Taking pictures of Tank's body using the MRI machine wasn't a necessity. Mariam wanted to take the X-rays or get a CT scan at her veterinary hospital, as it was strictly for animals and better suited for animals like mountain gorillas, especially for Tank. He was special and had his own room whenever he had visited the hospital over the years.

Once Tank had been settled in, he was wheeled over to the CT scanner for a few pictures to make sure he hadn't ruptured his stomach muscle or broken any ribs. Once that was done, they'd wheel him back to his room for observation.

Now that it was quiet and most of the veterinary hospital guests sleeping, Mariam used her stethoscope once again to see if she could hear that strange sound again. She placed her stethoscope onto Tank's stomach and over to his heart. Lo and behold, the sound was faint, but she believed she had heard it. A second heartbeat.

She shook her head "no," not believing what she had heard. She checked again. And again. And yet again. She checked like one does when checking the oil stick on one's car engine. One does it over and over again, making sure the stick shows "full."

After checking the sound many times over and over again, she still wasn't convinced about what she had heard. She decided to examine the CT image and see what she could find. Looking it over with a fine-toothed comb, she couldn't believe what she now saw. It was no bigger than a newborn mouse. She still couldn't believe what she was thinking.

Since the day of Tank's surgery back in Rwanda on that fateful day, she had been convinced that Tank was a male, even though his mid-section and groin area had been so badly damaged and mangled. The lack of the right equipment in the fire-damaged hospital to properly understand the extent of his injuries at the time hadn't helped. She had never even thought to look for ovaries or female organs, believing the baby wouldn't survive the surgery anyway. So, when she and her husband had operated on the baby gorilla, believing it to be a male, they had gone about fixing the mangled parts and the male parts they thought he was missing.

And over the years, she had updated the work she had done years before in Rwanda. His private parts, which she and George had rebuilt from scratch, had worked rather well, so she had figured if it wasn't broken, it didn't need fixing! So, she had left the repair alone.

And Tank's physicals that he needed to take for the three other sports teams were simple physicals consisting of listening to his heart, lungs, and breathing. That was it. The sports teams didn't want him to fail the physicals. He was a "Sports Phenom," as all the media named him. The real deal in every sport he played.

Mariam had to make sure that what she believed that sound to be would be confirmed when she looked at Tank's CT pictures. And just about the time she had seen her answer, she was sure that the radiologist at the hospital where Tank was first taken would look over their MRI images for any injuries Tank might have sustained. But Mariam wasn't really sure if they had even gotten to the point of doing the MRI scan when Tank had been laid out on the MRI table. Had she gotten there in time? Or was she too late and had they been able to take one or two pictures before she could stop them? She couldn't be sure. But she was going to keep the secret.

Tank was a female. Tank was not a male, as they'd always thought he was. But she also saw the secret that Tank was carrying. Tank was with child. "He" was a "she," and "she" was about two months pregnant.

***

When Mrs. Boyagian told Tank the news, he was just as confused as his mother had been when she's first heard those strange sounds through her stethoscope. Now she knew for sure what those sounds were. They were the beating of a second heartbeat.

She began to wonder what would happen to Tank's playing days when his teams' owners heard this news. Would they reject Tank or would they act as though nothing had happened?

The Boyagians, including Tank's brothers, let those thoughts quickly leave their heads. They weren't worrying about that at this point. Instead, they just celebrated and were overjoyed that Tank would soon be bringing another Boyagian into the world in about six more months. Such a beautiful thing. Tank just hoped the Rams and Angels would feel the same way when they heard the good news.

The Boyagians thought they should wait a few months to figure things out before alerting the owners and news media about the pregnancy. They would have Tank's agent tell the Rams and Angels general managers that Tank had ruptured his stomach muscle, cracked a few ribs, and needed months of rest to heal and mend.

That evening, while resting at the Boyagian Animal Hospital, Tank's mother came into his room to check up on him and say goodnight before leaving for home.

Tank had the television on, when a special report came on the screen. It was about Tank and his injuries. It seemed that someone in the radiology department at the first hospital Tank had been taken to had now leaked Tank's medical information to the press. Giving out medical information on a patient without proper authorization was actually illegal, but legality wasn't the important issue at this time. Tank would now face many additional problems beyond his injuries.

Before the media could overrun the hospital and its parking lot with their big semi-trucks, cameras, and crews, the Boyagians decided to get Tank out of there. He wasn't "in Kansas" anymore. They had to take him home to get him away from the interlopers and figure out how to deal with Tank's agent, the owners, and the general managers of the sports teams he had signed with. His brothers would have to deal with the feedback from Tank's sponsors and the manufacturers and companies that made Tank's memorabilia and shoes.

Tank and the Boyagians got out of the hospital just in time. As they were leaving the parking lot, the semi-trucks full of camera equipment, satellite dishes, and media crews were just pulling into the hospital. And when they had arrived at their home just minutes away from the hospital, camera crews were already setting up their equipment across the street.

Chapter 19

Now that it was known that Tank wasn't a male but was a female and pregnant, would the teams allow Tank to continue playing or would she be suspended from both teams or from just one team? If so, from which one? Baseball or football? But if they allowed her to play, would Tank be as dominant and the "Sports Phenom" that she had been after having the child? Only time would tell on both. And did Tank even want to continue to play? Those were just some of the questions the press wanted answered. Tank was the talk of the town. Again!

The female sports fans thought it was a beautiful thing that a "Sports Phenom" was having another little "Sports Phenom" that they all could watch grow up in the public spotlight, just like Tank had, starting in Midget football and going all the way up to the NFL, NBA, NHL, and MLB. Tank had put Los Angeles on the map!

The fans flipped both sides of the coin. The naysayers thought Tank had cheated them by being female and not male, and they believed all Tank's sports records should be erased.

On the other side of the coin were the sports fanatics who believed Tank should be allowed to play both sports, even if she was a female. Her talent shouldn't falter just because she had a child. If it did, then she should be released from the teams. But to do it beforehand didn't seem fair. That would be discrimination. And Tank had rights.

The emails and radio talk shows showed that 99 percent of the people supported Tank, even with child. They wanted to see another "Sports Phenom" grow up in front of their eyes to see if it—boy or girl—would be as good as Tank in the sports arena. Very few people who called into the sports talk shows or sent emails were against Tank and didn't want a female to play sports of any kind.

One caller asked a question that nobody had asked before. The man wanted to know who the father was who had gotten Tank pregnant, and if he had any sports background.

The Boyagians also wanted to know that answer, but they were certain, after speaking with the zoo's caretakers, that the father was the silverback gorilla. He was the only dominant male, so he would have fathered Tank's child. They figured Tank became pregnant when she taught class at the zoo. That's why the silverback had been so friendly with Tank when they had first met, rather than fighting to assert dominance. They had been friends from the get-go.

The zoo keepers had been stumped by the lack of any fighting. Now they knew why no fight had ever ensued.

They would know for certain, with a DNA test on the baby, whether their silverback was the father. The zoo was tickled pink to know that their silverback could produce children.

Now, they wondered if he had impregnated any of the other gorillas that had been sent by zoos from around the world to learn sign language. The zoo's press and promotion team would have to make some phone calls to see if any of those gorillas had gotten pregnant around the time they had visited the LA zoo.

The teams that Tank held contracts with were having a hard time deciding what to do. The Rams were in a dilemma. The NFL needed Tank in the game. She had brought the ratings up over 60 percent in the big cities and over 90 percent in local and rural areas. And she was bringing in over 200 million dollars to the league from sponsors every week.

The Rams had two choices. They could either release Tank outright and ban her from the game altogether, in which case they would lose everything Tank had gained for them. Or they could suspend her until the baby was born so as not to harm the fetus. In the meantime, Goodell would once again amend the NFL's constitution to allow either male or female gorillas to play on their teams. They wanted Tank to continue breaking records over and over again so that they could keep their goose that laid the golden eggs. They had everything to lose if they let her go, and everything to gain if they kept Tank on the team.

Goodell would have to meet with the owners and hear what they had to say . . . again.

The Angels, on the other hand, had no problem with Tank playing, male or female, pregnant or not. It made no difference as long as the MLB's Commissioner Robert Manfred Jr. signed off on it. And by the time Tank was due to give birth, the baseball season would be nearing Opening Day, just in time for Tank to break her home run record of 68 in a season. The fans knew Tank was ready to hit 70 home runs or better this season. But, of course, Manfred would have to meet with the owners of baseball franchises and have them sign off on the deal.

They also saw the signs of better things to come if Tank stayed in the game. They were facing the same dilemma as the Rams were. They knew how valuable Tank was to the league. Ratings were up more than 80 percent for the Angels and were even higher when they were playing in other ballparks.

***

The news media were stepping on each other's feet, vying for the best spot to get a picture of Tank's belly to see how big it had gotten. They believed the fetus to be almost three months old, which meant Tank would be due just around spring training.

Taking a month off for parental leave would give Tank enough time to get healthy enough to play baseball. The Angels were hoping she'd be ready to play by Opening Day.

After meeting with the owners, the NFL and Goodell explained to their fans why they'd had to suspend Tank from playing football but only until she had the baby. They claimed they didn't want the rough play of football to harm the fetus. Goodell promised to bring Tank back to the NFL and the Rams after the birth, but only if Tank wanted to return. They believed she might want to be a stay-at-home parent to her baby instead of playing on the gridiron.

Millions of Tank's fans hoped that would be the case. Tank had over 3 million Rams' fans but she also had over 20 million animal lovers who were also fans, knowing she was an endangered species. They wanted to witness the birth of the baby. They wanted to be in the birthing room to see the moment of birth and after.

When the Boyagians learned of the animal lovers' interest in Tank's pregnancy and birth, Mariam Boyagian promised them, in an interview with an LA Times reporter, that she would do her best to grant their wishes and videotape Tank weekly during her pregnancy and while giving birth.

This was a very big deal for the Boyagians, for Tank, and for tens of millions of his fans, as well as for the LA Zoo, where Tank had taught the other mountain gorillas to sign. The zoo advertised the silverback, whom they believed was the father. They would know for certain through DNA testing once Tank had given birth.

The news media didn't move for more than six months, waiting for any photos of Tank and her pregnancy. They vowed to stay until birth and possibly longer depending on the storyline.

They camped out and waited over five months, through the fall and winter, and nearing the end of February Tank had her baby, a four pound, four ounce healthy baby boy.

George and Mariam were now proud grandparents and Tank's brothers were now proud uncles. The family was as giddy as a bunch of school kids. Tank was giddy too, but in a quiet way. She was tired after being in labor for two days before giving birth.

The birth had been videotaped and sent via the internet on Tank's Facebook page for her fans to view.

Tank's fans were tickled pink watching the birth of an endangered species whose mother was smarter than many human beings. And she was sure to pass that intelligence from her to her boy. They also wondered if the baby would grow up to be another "Sports Phenom" as the Sports Writers had called Tank beginning at age five and continuing to present day.

The question now was whether Tank would rejoin her teammates for spring training by Opening Day or sooner. The Angels' fans were chomping at the bit to hear whether Tank would be in an Angels' uniform by or even before Opening Day.

It seemed as though that Tank's fans weren't interested in her baseball play. They were more interested in watching her motherly instincts and her nursing abilities as a new mother who had not grown up around her own species.

When the baby was older, Tank and the baby would be allowed to visit the zoo and let the father smell and touch his new baby. They wanted to see his reaction when Tank signed to tell him he was the father.

Chapter 20

Tank was a great mother even though she had been westernized and couldn't remember being nursed by her real mother with real milk. She only remembered the baby formula. But she would see to it that her infant would nurse even if she had to take him to the baseball stadium. He would have special steel mesh covers over both his stroller and basinet (just in case a baseball or football came whizzing at him) and Hazel would watch him on the sidelines or in the dugout while Tank played the game.

When Tank was asked by a reporter if she would be ready to play baseball by Opening Day, she replied in the affirmative, giving a "thumbs up." She wasn't asked about playing football because the season was still over seven months away. Tank's fans were sure she would also play and suit up for the Rams being that her boy would be seven months older.

That was Tank's plan for the future. She hadn't given up playing sports. She needed and wanted to honor her contracts and spring training would be starting in less than a month .

This baseball season, Tank finally made it to spring training by mid-March. The only difference was that

Tank came with her baby. While Tank was dressing, Hazel brought the little one to the dugout in a little bassinet with a mesh shield on it that didn't sit flat but was convex and about six inches high.

Tank came onto the field in her brand-new uniform that seemed smaller than last years' uniform. But it wasn't the uniform at all. Tank had gained weight, almost 30 pounds, since having the baby. She had gone from 505 pounds to 535 pounds . Her teammates wondered if Tank was the same player she had been the previous year. The manager and fans expected Tank to get them to the Promised Land. They were sure she'd get them to the World Series this year.

Tank walked to the batting cage and it seemed like "déjà vu" as his teammates gathered around the cage and waited to see if Tank had lost her edge due to having a baby.

While Tank was getting ready to play baseball, the NFL owners were whining again, even before knowing whether Tank would ever play football again. But Goodell wanted their blessing to amend the NFL's constitution again. This time, however, they added a female mountain gorilla to the amendment so that Tank would be allowed to play in the NFL. So now they were allowing both male and female mountain gorillas to play for the NFL. But to get the owners to agree, Goodell had had to make concessions concerning Tank.

The whining owners were using the same excuse— that Tank was "too good." But instead of banning Tank, like they had before, they compromised. Tank could only play two quarters for the team, but not the fourth quarter. She could play quarters one and two, or two and three or one and three, just not the fourth. They believed that would make it a little fairer for the opposing team. Goodell agreed to the compromise and the amendment to the constitution passed.

***

Tank entered the batting cage with her special bat. She stood at the plate. Before taking a pitch, she bent down, grabbed a handful of dirt, and rubbed it between her hands before throwing it back down to the ground. Now she was ready for the pitch. Tank's teammates wondered if she was still the "Sports Phenom" or if she would fizzle out at the plate. Within a few minutes, they had their answer.

While waiting for the pitch, Tank took a couple of practice swings, only swatting air. Then the pitch came across the plate at 98 mph, and just as fast, Tank sent it over the left field fence, thirty rows deep. The next pitch went over the centerfield wall at over 430 feet.

It seemed that Tank's weight wasn't a factor. Tank just seemed to have more power. The ball got out of the park faster than it had in the previous season.

After putting two dozen balls over the fences to all fields, Tank walked out to the pitcher's mound and threw the ball to see if she had lost any velocity on her fastball. Would her additional weight help or hinder? That was the question.

The news media finally were allowed to enter the field to watch Tank's practice. They missed Tank's batting practice, but were told by the teammates that Tank had even more power than the year before.

The cameras were allowed to photograph Tank and his teammates as long as they didn't become a nuisance. They also wanted to photograph Tank's baby and got the chance when Hazel held him in her arms close to her chest. His head was close to hers, as she patted him on the back to help him sleep. The photographers kept the baby awake with the clicking sounds of their cameras. They had not been told the baby's name, so Hazel told them that the Boyagian's grandbaby was named after the Chicago Bears defensive tackle and fullback William "Refrigerator/Fridge" Perry.

That was a first for the media and their reporters couldn't get to their phones fast enough to report to their studios and email them the photos and name of Tank's baby.

Baseball was going great for the Angels. Tank started where she had left off. And while they had off days at home, Tank talked Hazel into driving her to the zoo to show the father and the rest of the class her baby.

The zookeepers watched the interactions with the other gorillas. However, they evidently didn't watch closely enough, because nearly seven months later, Tank was feeling poorly and selected to sit out the game. When the trainer checked her out in the locker room, first with his stethoscope to check all of Tank's vitals, he heard two strange sounds—a second and a third heartbeat. He used an ultrasound device, and it verified the stethoscope sounds. Tank was pregnant with twins and due in only one month. So, Tank's baseball season was over.

The baseball season was nearly over, but Tank had gotten to the playoffs. But without Tank's power in the lineup, the Angels had lost in the second round, so their season was over now, too.

Now, Tank, Hazel, and the baby walked out to the players' parking lot. Before they reached Hazel's car, the four Indonesian gangsters surprised them. Tank saw the gun one of the gangsters had pointed at them. To save Hazel and the baby, Tank fought hard and beat three of them, but the fourth shot her in the chest and head, killing her instantly.

The gangsters tried to get away, but the Stadium's security guards had seen what was happening and fired back. Gunfire rang out, and when it was all over, the four Indonesian gangsters were either dead or dying. Five minutes later, all had succumbed to their injuries.

Tank was rushed to the hospital to try and save the twins, but it wasn't to be. The two fetuses had died with their mother. And so did the Angels' and Rams' hopes of winning with Tank.

When the news media heard what had happened to Tank and that she had died, that was it for them. Now, there was no reason to stay across the street from the Boyagian house. They packed up their gear, threw it all into the semi-truck, and left for the next hot story. But not before they videotaped Tank's funeral. More than 100,000 fans came to her funeral, and most came out crying. They loved Tank. The mountain gorilla was more than a Sports Phenom to them. Tank had helped put LA on the map. It was a sad day for all.

The dreams of the Rams and Angels' owners faltered with the death of Tank and the twins.

***

As the years passed by, the Boyagians were no sixlonger bothered by the news media. Nearly five years had passed since that fateful day. Tank's son, Refrigerator, was nearly five years old and nothing was set in his life. Although the Rams had signed Refrigerator to a contract when he was born, and Tank had approved it, they really didn't know if "Fridge" would ever take Tank's place. They were just playing the odds.

While nobody was watching, Refrigerator picked up one of his mini-footballs that his mother and uncles used to throw when they were his age. Outside, in the back yard, he threw a perfect spiral pass nearly 30 yards.

The End

Epilog

Only time would tell if the Boyagians had another "Sports Phenom" in their midst. Would Refrigerator take after his mother in sports and in teaching sign language? Only time would tell. Read Monkey Football 2 and find out.